MW01244424

The Running Path

The Running Path

by Lisa M. Miller

Editor: Marsha Briscoe
Printed in the United States of America

Published by
WHISKEY CREEK PRESS LLC
Whiskeycreekpress.com

Copyright © 2010 by: Lisa M. Miller

Warning: The unauthorized reproduction or distribution of this copyrighted work is illegal. Criminal copyright infringement, including infringement without monetary gain, is investigated by the FBI and is punishable by up to 5 (five) years in federal prison and a fine of $250,000.

Names, characters and incidents depicted in this book are products of the author's imagination or are used fictitiously. Any resemblance to actual events, locales, organizations, or persons, living or dead, is entirely coincidental and beyond the intent of the author or the publisher.

No part of this book may be reproduced or transmitted in any form or by any means, electronic or mechanical, including photocopying, recording, or by any information storage and retrieval system, without permission in writing from the publisher.

Print ISBN: 978-1-60313-975-5

Dedication

I would like to thank my husband, family and friends for their continuous love, support and guidance; and to God for these blessings. This book is for Christian and Stephen; hoping they grow up to love reading and writing as much as their mom. And as promised, Dad, the first copy is reserved for you.

Chapter 1

The engine in Paul's car screamed as he pushed the limits of his Volkswagen. He crested the top of the hill and slowed as he approached the house. It was just as he expected: the front lawn was littered with neighbors waiting for an explanation. They milled around like grazing cattle but perked up when someone walked out of the home. The sight of a police cruiser and an ambulance positioned in front of the home provoked many stares and whispers. When sirens pierced the air and the reflection of red and blue lights danced against windowpanes, the people of Watertown wanted to know what was disrupting their little Adirondack community.

Paul ran his finger over the metal coil on his notebook down to its jagged edge. He pushed the razor end inward and tucked the notebook into his pocket. He was uneasy about attempting to do this. Interviewing people in this type of situation wasn't the usual procedure, but even if he didn't talk to anyone, he could observe the emotion first hand.

The porch creaked with each step as he approached the immense officer guarding the door.

"Are you with the Jensen family?" the policeman questioned.

"No, my name is Paul Triver from WWNY-TV."

"Listen, only family and close friends are allowed in there," the officer said. "We don't need any news people running around, upsetting them even more."

Paul strained to peer over the man's shoulder and noticed the paramedics lifting a sheet-covered body onto a stretcher. The crisp whiteness was contrasted greatly by the deep red that permeated the top of the sheet. There was a flurry of paramedics while others in the house tried to console one another. A woman wailed as the lifeless form was placed on a gurney and wheeled out to the porch. Paul watched as they placed the body, now zipped into a gray canvas bag, into the back of a vehicle. Outside, shaking heads and whispered words continued.

"Can I just ask what happened?" Paul inquired.

The officer squinted into the distance. He studied the tip of his worn, black boot and paused before answering. His heavy coat rustled against Paul's sleeve as he leaned towards him. The pungent smell of tobacco and coffee grew even stronger as he disclosed his knowledge of the situation.

"That poor woman in there came home to find her fourteen-year-old daughter shot in the head, lying in a pool of blood. Now, like I said, this is not a good time to be poking around asking questions. I think you were here long enough," he said, motioning towards the steps.

Paul was satisfied that he didn't get chased away sooner. He thanked the officer for his information and headed back to his car. The mournful sobbing could still be heard from within the house.

Chapter 2

The thermometer barely registered with its miniscule two degrees. Despite the frigid temperatures, Abby decided to walk to work. Her resolution for the New Year was to incorporate more exercise into her lifestyle, but it was almost February and her resolve was faltering. When she stepped outside, she knew she should have put it off another day. The biting cold made her face numb and the wind caused her eyes to tear.

She walked several blocks until the sight of the familiar storefront up ahead pushed her to sprint the remaining distance. Bells rattled against the glass from her struggle in closing the door.

"Hi there, Jeb," Abby called. She threw her bag on the glass counter and peeled her gloves off her frozen hands. The cozy store gave her some relief. "I am still trying to figure out why I walked today."

"Yeah, cold morning, but I have the perfect solution for you: how does a hot coffee and fresh banana nut muffin sound?" Jeb asked as he pointed to the glass-covered platter. No matter what kind of morning Abby was having, she had to smile when she saw Jeb: the white apron coordinating well with his silvery hair and his pudgy fingers always busy preparing something that looked incredible, even though it wouldn't rate too high on the health scale.

"Mmmm, that sounds good, but I really shouldn't. I am trying to watch what I eat. Just the paper, and make it a large coffee today," she replied.

Jeb shook his head and placed her paper in front of her. He turned to pour the coffee, while she performed her daily ritual scanning the headlines.

He placed the Styrofoam cup in front of her, along with a small container. Abby knew she wasn't getting out of there without one of the muffins. She tucked the paper into her bag and made room for the tempting, aromatic pastry. After putting on her defenses again from the cold, she grabbed her coffee and headed towards the door.

"See ya, Jeb, and thanks…but I just want to let you know that you are not helping with my New Year resolution," she said.

Jeb shrugged his shoulders and smiled.

As she pushed against the front door and met the bitter wind outside, she tried to figure out how many days until spring. By the time she got to the station's front entrance, she was frozen again. Her glove-covered hands made it awkward to juggle everything and fumble with her key. Just as she was about to throw everything onto the ground, the weight of her bag was lifted, and she heard a familiar voice offering to help.

"Hi, Paul. Thanks," she said and stepped back to let him open the door.

"Good morning. How are you?" Paul asked.

"Okay, and you?" she replied. It had only been a few months since Paul started at WWNY. It is not that Abby resented that his career change brought him to Watertown, but that he jumped in as a reporter right from the start. She had been working as the assignment desk editor for over a year. She realized that Paul did intern and work in a larger market previously, but it was hard when she had her heart set on something and the new guy just jumps right into it instead.

After her morning small talk with Paul, she sat at one of the computer workstations. She watched as he meticulously placed his folders in a neat stack on the corner of his desk. He truly loved his job and was one of the most organized people Abby had ever met. She envied that quality. His confidence, personality, and approach with people always put others at ease. This was all in addition to his stunning smile and wavy brown hair.

"Any news?" he asked.

"No, nothing that wasn't mentioned last night," she said.

One of the hardest parts of the job was trying to create news when there was none. Unless she had a breaking story, Abby often struggled to put a full newscast together. There was a call the other day about stolen skis at Gore Mountain; *that* was the excitement during her shift. Abby skimmed through last night's stories for follow-ups while lending a trained ear to the scanners. From the minute she walked in the door, the annoying pitch and squelch of the police scanners resonated throughout the room. She listened for anything newsworthy.

"Look in the obituaries; see if there is a listing for *Jensen, Christa Jensen*," Paul said.

Abby flipped to the center of *The Watertown Daily Times* and scanned the page for the name while sipping her reliably strong coffee. "No, I don't see anything. Why, what happened?" she asked.

Before Paul could answer, in walked Dave Harris, the station's news director for a little over a year.

"Hi, guys, good morning," Dave greeted as he strode past them, balancing books and a coffee thermos. He walked into his small office and Abby watched as he placed his stuff on the desk before coming back out into the newsroom. For as organized as Paul was, Dave was the opposite. At least a few hundred newspaper clippings littered his desk and some were tacked to the walls.

"Did you hear about the Jensen girl? I know it wasn't in the paper, but my sister knows the family. It's a shame, but it will tie into our idea. Did you hear about it, Paul?" Dave asked. He may have been a bit scattered and hyper, but he was an intelligent man. He could never sit still. He leaned against the corner of the desk, absent-mindedly pulling and snapping the loose strip that was peeling away from the edge. He stopped when he noticed Paul glancing at his hand.

"Yeah, I heard the call on the scanner the other day. I was just about to leave when I heard it come over. I know it is not policy to cover things like that, but I thought that if I got a feel for the place where it happened and maybe talked to someone who knew Christa that it would be helpful," Paul said.

"Any luck?" Dave asked.

"No, but I plan on going back there in a few days. Just before you walked in, I was starting to ask Abby about it."

"Oh yeah, tell her what's going on," Dave said as he went back to his office.

That was one thing Abby didn't care for: there seemed to be camaraderie between the two that she wasn't privileged to be part of.

"What did you want to tell me?" she asked before Paul even had a chance to start talking.

"Oh, Dave wanted us to do a short series focusing on teens in the area. I figured you might want to help me out. It could be good experience."

Abby was surprised that he was including her. She was always looking for something that would enhance her resume. Paul had her attention.

"Sure, what's it about?" she asked. Not that she would refuse to do it, but she was just curious.

"Well, we were thinking of illustrating different aspects of teen life and problems they have to deal with. Christa Jensen was a fourteen-year-old girl that lived in Lowville. Her mother came home to discover her body. They found the gun next to her; she shot herself in the head. The poor family, they are not taking it very well. But who would? Can you imagine someone that young committing suicide? You really don't think things like that happen around here, but I guess they do, right? Abby?"

She didn't hear the last part of Paul's story. The word *suicide* stopped everything around her. She just stared down at her computer monitor.

Paul tried to talk to her again. Her fingers grasped the base of her neck as she lowered her head. She tried to clear the images from her mind.

"Hey, are you listening to me?" he asked, realizing that Abby was zoned out.

She sat back in her seat and apologized. "I'm sorry; I'm just not with it today. Yeah, you're right, though, it is sad. That's so young. Are you sure you want to go over there to talk to the family? Usually the media doesn't publicize something like that, especially because of the young age." She did not want to venture into this project and was hoping she could get out of it somehow.

"It's not about her specific suicide; it's about suicide in general. Maybe some information could even help other families to see warning signs. It's still in the rough stages, but don't you think it sounds like a great idea?"

"Yeah, just great," Abby said.

She turned to her computer and started scrolling through last night's run down sheet. She glanced over and was relieved to see that Paul had moved over to talk to Dave. They were both talking, nodding their heads in agreement about something Paul was showing Dave in the newspaper. Dave again nodded in agreement. Of course, everyone listened to Paul. He always had the great ideas.

Just as Abby was about to make herself scarce, the two of them came over to the desk.

"Hey, Ab, I think it's great that you'll be working on this with Paul. It will be good experience for you," Dave said as he patted her on the back, causing her to wince.

Abby realized that between Paul and Dave, they had made up her mind for her. Actually, she was surprised that Paul didn't want to work on this himself. "Yeah, it should be good experience," she replied with very little enthusiasm.

She looked back at her screen, trying to seem busy. As much as this situation bothered her, she knew that in the world of reporting, she was faced with upsetting factors in life everyday. If she ever planned on making it out of Watertown, she couldn't turn down opportunities like this…even if it was with Mr. Personality and about a subject she wished she would never hear about again.

"Does that sound good?" Dave asked.

"What was that?" Abby inquired, having zoned out again.

"I said that we should probably go tomorrow afternoon to talk to Mrs. Jensen," Paul restated.

"I will talk to you guys later," Dave said. He walked back into his office, plopping down in his leather chair and immediately picking up the phone.

Abby twirled her pen with her fingers, trying to ignore the fact that he wanted her to interview Mrs. Jensen. She clicked the ballpoint several times, wondering if the repetitive noise was aggravating Paul.

"I thought you would be happy to work on this. Aren't you?" Paul asked.

"I don't know about happy, but yeah, I guess it will be good," she said. Abby really didn't feel like getting into the long explanation about why she was so hesitant to do this. "You don't think it's too soon to talk to the mother? I am sure the family is so devastated; I can't imagine that they are ready to talk about this."

"I talked to Mrs. Jensen earlier. She was surprised, too, that I called her. When I explained that I was inquiring not about her daughter's death but looking to see if there was anything we could do to prevent this from happening to someone else, I think it made sense to her. I pushed the fact that she would be helping other people out. I'd like to talk to her before she changes her mind. We'll go over tomorrow morning if that works with you."

"Who's going to watch the desk? I'm surprised Dave wants to let me venture into the light of day; I'm always cooped up in this office."

"Abby, if you don't want to do this, fine, but I just thought it would be a great opportunity for you. I thought maybe you could do some stand ups or something, but if you're not interested, I'll do it myself," Paul offered.

Abby could tell he was getting aggravated with her. She knew that she was being difficult, but considering the circumstances, she couldn't help it.

"No, no, I'm sorry. I'm happy to be given a chance to work on this. I really appreciate it. What time tomorrow?" she asked. She forced a weak smile, but it was enough to receive one in return from Paul.

"How about eight o'clock?"

"Sure, sounds good. I just have to finish up here. Today, I'm grasping at straws to find anything interesting," she said as she got back to her computer screen before Paul saw through her and started asking questions.

"Okay, I'll talk to you before you go," he said, patting her on the shoulder before he headed back to Dave's office.

Abby placed her head in her hands. Her mind was swimming with ideas and thoughts, mainly about how she was going to get through tomorrow.

She found a few stories to follow up on for future newscasts and placed them in the weekly folder. After the six o'clock broadcast, Abby gathered her things and planned on going home. She didn't want to discuss anything else with Paul. After shutting her monitor off, she tried to slither out of the newsroom. It looked like Paul was involved in something anyway. *Good,* she thought while pushing the door open. She knew that tomorrow would be difficult, and talking to Paul right now was not on her agenda.

A cold gust of wind blew the edge of the hallway carpet over her foot. The evening air stung her face. She pulled her woolen scarf close to her mouth, her warm breath giving her some solace from the biting cold. Abby wished that she had decided to drive her old, green Honda today. Her pace quickened across the parking lot.

Abby reached her street and couldn't wait to get home and relax. She never thought she would find a place as comforting as the home where she was raised, but this place came close. The structure housed only four apartments. Abby wasn't very close with her neighbors, but she was cordial when she greeted them. The best part of living in this area was the location. Although the Lake George region was rural in itself, many surrounding areas consisted of close-knit communities. Terrance Street was a dead end road, with Abby's home right at the end. She was minutes from downtown, but behind her house, the beautiful, tree-adorned landscape served as a great view from her bedroom window. She couldn't wait until the weather would break, so she could spend more time outdoors. The path behind her yard twisted through the woods, spilling out onto the other side of Watertown. During the summer months, she could find several people walking and running. Right now, there wasn't much snow on the ground, but it was still too cold to exercise outside.

She walked into her apartment and opened the refrigerator. The light illuminated the kitchen. She figured that it was the openness of the living space that made her the most comfortable. The far wall was lined with gray cabinets and appliances. The island directly across from it served as a room divider, eating area, and place to toss books, magazines, and mail. She stared at the half-full container of Chinese food, apples, and some leftover chicken and realized that she needed to stop at the store soon. She grabbed a bottle of water and settled for the piece of chicken. Usually, she would watch television until eleven o'clock and then go to sleep. It was very rare that she would stay up for the news, considering she knew everything that was going on from working with it all day. The last thing she wanted to do was to see it again. She looked at the clock and even though it was only ten, her repetitive yawning reminded her that she should catch up on her sleep.

Before settling down beneath her feather-filled comforter, she sat in the bow window. This was by far her favorite place in the apartment. Her dad always said that the window was the reason she decided on the place; however, it wasn't very well insulated, and the cold draft sent shivers through her body. Abby rested her forehead against the pane. It was cool against her skin. She stared out the window into the vast tangle of barren branches bordering her yard. The darkness only allowed faint moonlight to cast slight shadows behind her home.

On the far right side of the ledge where she sat was a small, white picture frame. Abby picked up the photo and smiled. They looked so happy in that picture. It brought back memories of summer. Even though there were many months until that serene season arrived, she could still vividly recall the treasured days they enjoyed. She placed the image of the two of them that captured that last day of school on her nightstand. No matter how many years passed, she still missed her friend.

After her second yawn, Abby figured she should retire for the night. Tomorrow would be a long day, but there was no backing out now. She let the soft, down-filled comforter envelope her body and thought about Mrs. Jensen and how she must be feeling tonight. She looked one last time at the picture that she moved next to her bed and cried herself to sleep.

Chapter 3

The buzzer on the alarm clock echoed its annoying shrill throughout the bedroom. It was early, but Abby was up several minutes before her clock alerted her. Usually, she would sleep as long as she could, but not today. She didn't want to do this interview, not even with Paul there.

Just as she was about to jump in the shower, the phone rang. It was Paul.

"Yes, I'm up," she muttered after being greeted by an all-too-chipper voice.

"You don't sound up. What's wrong? You still sound tired."

"God, Paul, it is six-thirty a.m.; what do you expect?" she responded after stifling a yawn. He was right, though; she was still tired. She may have awoken on her own, but that didn't change the fact that she was up several times throughout the night. Between her unsettling dreams that interrupted her sleep and her apprehension about today, she did not feel well-rested.

"Well, get ready; I will be over around a quarter to eight. This is the only time Mrs. Jensen could talk to us. She has to meet with a counselor later today," he said.

"All right, I'll be ready," Abby replied. She didn't understand why they had to do this so soon. In her mind, she thought it was still too early for this woman to talk about the suicide of her daughter...but they say talking about it helps. Abby really didn't think so.

The five outfits strewn across her disheveled bed didn't appeal to her this morning. She decided on a simple black sweater with tan dress pants. She was never totally satisfied with anything in her wardrobe, but this would have to do. Her budget did not allow for a vast or expensive clothing collection.

She fidgeted with her hair until she heard Paul beeping the horn outside. The reflection staring back at her was disappointing. Her straight, walnut brown hair never looked the way she wanted it to. She brushed on a coat of chocolate tinted lipstick and gently smudged her eyeliner. The smoky appearance she was shooting for would turn into raccoon eyes in a matter of hours anyway.

She grabbed her purse and black bag and headed out the door to find Paul standing outside of his Volkswagen.

"I was just about to come in to get you," he said as he walked around to the passenger side to open the door for Abby.

She paused for a moment, mainly because the gesture shocked her. Abby was not accustomed to politeness. The tumultuous relationship she ended a few months prior left some bitter feelings behind. Her friends warned her about her sorry excuse for a boyfriend, but it was too late by the time she realized what her friends tried to alert her about. After that emotional roller coaster, not only did she not date but also ended up alienating some of her friends. There was only one or two she would still talk to.

"Hello?" Paul called as he held the door.

Abby threw her bags in and slipped into the seat.

"Sorry, I am still half asleep," she said.

They drove over to the Jensen house, talking about work and the weather, but not bringing up anything about what they were going to do. They parked in front of a quaint home with a huge porch. Paul turned off the car and sat there instead of getting out. He turned to Abby.

"Are you ready?" he asked her.

She was hoping that he wouldn't notice her shaking hands.

"Don't worry, I'll ask most of the questions. Is that what you are nervous about?" he asked.

It wasn't, but Abby agreed. "Yeah, I guess. I am usually behind the scenes, you know. This is one of my first big assignments, especially with the illustrious Paul Triver." Abby tried to lighten the mood. She did not want to tell him the real reason she felt like she was ready to jump out of her skin.

"Oh, right, this is your first step in being a big time reporter," Paul joked.

As they walked up the steps, Abby could feel her heart pounding in her chest. She knew what to expect, but didn't know if she could handle it.

Mrs. Jensen must have anticipated their arrival. She swung the door open even before they approached the steps. Abby let Paul do the introductions.

"Hi, Mrs. Jensen. Paul Triver from WWNY," he said in a professional but soft-spoken voice. "And this is Abby Greene, one of our news editors."

Abby wiped her hand on the side of her pants before extending it towards Mrs. Jensen. It was sweaty and trembling; the anxiety and nervous state could not be hidden.

"Hi, it's nice to meet you both. Please come in and let me take your coats," Mrs. Jensen said. Her full face was inviting, but the smile seemed unnatural.

In just the few seconds of their introduction, Abby sensed so much sadness in the woman's eyes.

Mrs. Jensen muttered something from the other room about being thirsty and poked her head around the corner. "Water, soda, or coffee?" she asked, tapping her finger on the doorframe.

"Nothing for me, thanks. Do you want anything?" Paul asked Abby.

"Water is fine, thank you," she responded. Maybe she should have asked for something stronger at this point.

Abby watched Mrs. Jensen disappear again into the kitchen. Her short, cropped hair was a vibrant red. She wondered if Christa Jensen had red hair. She looked around the living room and noticed a cluster of picture frames on the table in the corner. She walked over and studied them. The young, smiling girl in the picture had a mane of cascading red locks that were identical in color to Mrs. Jensen. Most of the pictures were of this beautiful young girl, baby pictures and some that must have been recent. Paul was standing behind Abby, looking over her shoulder. The silence in the room was punctuated with the dull ticking of the grandfather clock in the hall.

"What a pretty girl," he whispered while looking at a picture of Christa. She was kneeling in a yard, with her arm around a big golden retriever. "It is such a shame."

"It is sad, it's really sad," Abby agreed while looking around the room. Pictures of the fair-skinned redhead adorned almost every wall and mantle. She must have been the only child. Abby shuddered at this thought.

"Here's some ice water for both of you." Mrs. Jensen entered, placing the tall glasses on top of the runner on the table. Mrs. Jensen picked up the pint tumbler and swirled its contents. A slice of bright yellow lemon settled on top of an equal sized piece of cucumber.

Abby was startled when she walked back in; she didn't want Mrs. Jensen to think they were snooping. Hiding her embarrassment, Abby sipped slowly, her parched throat receptive to the unusual but pleasant taste.

"Oh, sorry, we were just looking at the pictures of Christa. What a beautiful young lady," Abby said. "I'm so sorry about your loss."

"Yes, Mrs. Jensen, our deepest condolences. Please let me know if you think all of this is too soon. We can come back at a later time," Paul interjected.

Abby knew he didn't really want to cancel this interview, but she thought that after he walked in the house he felt a little uneasy, too.

"No, please, sit down," the woman said. "I am going through so many emotions right now and I feel better if I keep talking. I think I've told people what happened a million times. The problem is no matter how many times I say it, I still can't believe that my Christa is gone. Some of my neighbors told me not to talk to the television station and that it is too soon. But you are not going to just do a story on Christa, right?" she asked.

"No, we're not," Paul replied. "My partner and I are doing a series on teen issues and keeping the community informed of problems that they or their kids are facing. Maybe if this tragedy could be used as a tool to help someone else, it wouldn't make your daughter come back, but maybe it could prevent someone else from losing one."

He really sounds sincere, Abby thought. It was hard not to be soothed when she was in his presence. When he was concerned about something, he lowered his voice to just above a whisper then listened with great intent. His soulful eyes would stay with hers, while he would nod his head in agreement. Combine this with his appealing looks, and he could basically have anyone's attention. Abby saw this work on many people…and she didn't mean just making girls swoon; even some guys at the station had a respect for him. His personality and his deep concern for other people's problems made him a likable person. But Abby knew that around most women, his dark, wavy hair and deep cobalt eyes would hold their attention even with out his sparkling demeanor.

Mrs. Jensen seemed to be willing to share her feelings. She talked a lot about her daughter. She talked about her when she was a baby and in grade school. She made reference to the pictures setting next to them several times.

"How is Mr. Jensen?" Paul asked, trying discreetly to jot down notes.

"He's having a very hard time. It's usually quiet here at night. We don't like discussing it. Hopefully the therapy will help us with that. He is back to work today. Again, some people said it is too soon, but he said that he needed to get his mind off of everything. It was just such a blow to us," she said.

"That was one of my questions. Did you see any signs leading up to her death?" Paul asked.

"Well, now that I look back, I realized that there were signs, but I didn't see them when it mattered most. Christa was always a happy girl. She was involved in so many activities at school and had several friends. As you can see from the pictures, she was stunning. Last year, my husband's sister passed away. Christa was devastated; she was very close to her aunt and really admired her. I guess I should have sent her for counseling, but we figured it was going to take her a long time to deal with her grief. After a few months, she seemed to have no interest in her usual activities. She started gaining weight after consoling herself for months with food. We tried to talk to her and suggested taking her to speak to someone professionally, but she always refused. We should have insisted. She kept withdrawing and was quiet at dinner. Teens go through these stages, plus her aunt's death just made things even harder. Now we realize that she was depressed." Mrs. Jensen crumbled and ripped the tissue that was falling apart in her hands. Her lips started to tremble. "You don't realize what I am going through over and over in my head." She paused again, completely shredding the tissue, the pieces falling to the floor like snow. "She was crying out for help and we didn't listen. I just wish I had tried something else, but we just never thought that she would kill herself," she said, trying to hold back tears. "You can't imagine how I felt walking into the living room, finding my little girl dead." With that, she lost it. She dug the heel of her palms into her eyes, her chest heaving with uncontrollable sobs.

"Mrs. Jensen, please, you don't have to continue," Paul consoled as he walked over to get her some more tissues.

During this entire time, Abby's breath was becoming more and more shallow. Her face was hot, and her sweat-soaked shirt was plastered to her back. She was swooning and had to get out of the room. Tears were welling up in her eyes as she tried to stand. Paul looked over at her and frowned. She got up and knocked the dining room chair over in her haste.

"Mrs. Jensen, I'm sorry, I just can't…" Abby said, stumbling over the words.

She broke into tears before she even reached the door and ran out to the car as fast as she could. The door was locked, so she leaned against it and tried to stop crying. She felt ridiculous breaking down like that, but she knew it was going to happen. She watched as Mrs. Jensen stood at the door talking to Paul. She wiped her eyes then tucked the tissue in her pocket. She shook Paul's hand and touched his shoulder. She looked out at Abby and gave a slight smile and little wave. Abby reciprocated then turned away.

She heard Paul's shoes crunching on the gravel. He had Abby's coat draped over his arm. He came up behind her and with a firm gentleness, squeezed her arms.

"Are you okay?"

"Can we just go?" she asked, still sniffling. Her face burned from the wind chapping her tear soaked cheeks.

"Yeah. Here, let me get that," he said, unlocking the door.

As they pulled away, he waved again to Mrs. Jensen. The steady hum of the car was the only sound filtering around them. After about five minutes of driving, he asked Abby what was wrong and if she wanted to talk about it.

She looked down at her lap, wringing her hands. She knew that what happened back there was going to need an explanation. "Paul, I have to tell you something," she began. Abby didn't know where to start. It all felt fresh again, like she was going through the horrid experience one more time. The peaceful memories she recalled last night were replaced by the horrid images playing over and over again.

She didn't say anything for a while. Paul respected that. He answered her with the same tense silence. Abby stared out the window, focusing her attention on everything but the subject at hand. Her eyes followed the length of crooked wire fence, a dented moose crossing sign, and acres of barren woods. The sky looked ominous, but Abby wished it would just swallow her out of this situation. Even several years later, it haunted her. She thought about it often, but struggled to push it to the back of her mind. Talking about it sometimes made it easier to handle, but not easier to understand.

Paul looked over at her. "Do you want to stop at the diner up here?" he asked.

She knew the little greasy spoon he was talking about. Coffee seemed liked a good idea right now. It was past the time that the breakfast crowd filled the ripped, vinyl booths of Clara's Diner. This should give them some privacy and a chance to talk.

"Yeah, that sounds good. Paul, listen, I'm really sorry about what happened back there. I know it wasn't professional, but I just couldn't help it," she apologized.

Her body started to fill with anxiety again, and Paul sensed it. "Let's get something to eat; you don't have to explain anything now."

Paul pulled in front of the diner. From the looks of the amount of cars in front of the small, aluminum trailer, they would be the only two patrons.

Abby didn't say anything as they walked through the door and were seated. Paul helped her with her coat and hung it next to his on the rusted metal pole jutting up from the corner of the bench chair. Immediately, the waitress came over to take their order.

"I will just have coffee and a banana nut muffin, if you have it," she said, not even looking at the menu.

"Coffee, for me, and the two egg special, scrambled," he ordered, smiling at the woman.

"So, what did you need to tell me?" he asked after the waitress left.

"It's a long story, a very long story," Abby said.

Before she started unraveling her history, the waitress returned with two blue-rimmed ceramic cups. The piping hot coffee was overflowing onto the saucer as she placed them in front of the two. She turned to Paul and asked if he wanted cream and sugar.

"No, black is fine. Abby?" he asked.

"Cream and sugar, please," she said.

Abby made her coffee almost white with cream and saturated with sweetener then settled back into the booth. "So, you probably think I am an idiot, right?" she asked.

"Why would you say that? I just didn't know what was going on back there. Were you that upset about Christa Jensen? It's sad, but you have to try to separate your emotions from your work. I saw that you were rattled, but I knew that this was your first story like this. It's hard."

Paul was trying to sound compassionate, but he was also lecturing her. Abby knew she should clue him in as to what was going on.

"Listen, did I ever tell you about Becca? My friend from years ago?" she asked.

"No, not that I recall. Do you still talk to her?"

"No, I don't. She's dead," Abby retorted, with a bit of sarcasm in her voice.

The waitress's perfect timing interrupted their conversation. Paul buttered his toast as the waitress asked if they needed anything else.

"No we're fine, thanks," he said.

"I'm sorry, Ab, I didn't know. What happened?" he asked after the waitress walked away.

Abby started with some background information. "When I was growing up, I had several friends, but no one that I was extremely close to. Then, the spring when I just turned twelve, I met Becca. She moved here not long before that. She lived with her Uncle Jonathan and Aunt Theresa. Her mother died months earlier from cancer."

"My God. How tragic. What about her father?" Paul asked, not even touching his breakfast.

"Her father left the family when she was very young. They weren't very close to the extended family. The grandmother, Colin's mother, offered to help with Jean and her young daughter, but Becca's mother wanted nothing to do with his side of the family after he deserted them. This left Jean's only brother, Jonathan. She wasn't particularly close to him, but she needed someone to say that they would take care of Becca if she lost her fight with cancer. Things were going well, and they thought that the cancer went into remission. But late in the school year, Jean's fight ended. Becca was devastated that now she not only lost her father but a mother as well. Begrudgingly, she moved in with her aunt and uncle. They weren't used to having children around the house, but they did the best they could to accommodate Becca." Abby paused to break a piece off her muffin and sip the now tepid coffee.

"That is sad, but how did she die?" Paul asked.

Abby could see that he was truly interested in her story, whether it was the reporter in him or true concern. She had his full attention.

"Anyway, to make a long story longer, we met at the end of that school year and clicked right away. We were inseparable that summer. I would either stay at her uncle's house or she would stay at mine. We were both only children, and we had everything in common. That summer, my family planned a camping trip not far from our home. I begged Becca to come with us, but she said that I should just go with my family. She said that I didn't spend enough time with them, and she should spend some time with her uncle since he and her aunt were so generous.

"It turned into the worst vacation of my life. Everything was going well up until the last few days of our trip. After spending the day on the lake, I returned to the cabin we rented. My mother was crying as I walked inside. I thought it was something to do with my dad. I asked her what was wrong and she sat me down and told me what had happened back at home. The campsite office clerk received the phone call and relayed the terrible news to my mother. Without hesitating, we raced back to Watertown and drove immediately to the Rices'. The short drive seemed to have taken hours. As soon as I arrived at the house, I ran into the living room to find Jonathan and Theresa holding each other and crying. When they noticed me standing there, Jonathan held me next to him and said he was sorry I had to go through this. I broke away and ran upstairs towards Becca's room. A man was standing next to her bed. It must have been the doctor. There were several people there. The only thing that stands out in my mind was the lifeless form on the bed covered with the sheet. A gurney was next to the frilly pink four-poster bed, waiting to transport the small body. She was covered with a sheet, but her small feet peeked out from the bottom. I recognized the pink polish that she always painted her fingers and toes with. Then, I lost it. My mother ran upstairs and beckoned me to come down to the living room." Again, all of this emotion brought back the horrid memories, causing Abby to break down again. "I'm sorry Paul," she said, digging through her purse for a tissue.

"Here." Paul handed her a napkin. "You don't have to go any further."

"No, I'll finish. Basically, it was discovered that Becca took an overdose of painkillers that she found in the house. The Rices found her in her bedroom with a bottle of pills next to her bed. There was no note, no explanation. And that was it: my best friend was gone and I had no answers. I still have no answers. There was no indication of her being depressed, no clues. I just don't know what went wrong or what I could have done to prevent it. I constantly think that there was more that I could have done. It just didn't make any sense."

Paul leaned over the table and held Abby's hands. He whispered, "I'm sorry. You don't have to explain anything else. I know why this is hard for you and I apologize that I forced you into this."

Abby appreciated his sincerity. "You didn't force me into anything. I wanted to do it. I knew it would be hard, but I think working on this will help me. Maybe if I help someone else, it will help me."

"Well, whatever decision you make, please let me know. If you want to work on the story, fine. If not, I will understand. Remember, I will always be around to talk."

Abby stared at Paul's piercing blue eyes. He was definitely Paul talking as a friend, not as a reporter. She appreciated that. "Thank you."

Chapter 4

Jeremy Greish looked at his watch. It looked like they were only going to have time for one more run. He turned around and looked for his friend. He saw him weaving his way down the intimidating mountain with what seemed little effort. Paul stopped only inches from him, spraying the granular snow against Jeremy. Although he knew they had to go soon, he was hoping they could get a few more runs in.

"How about one or two more?" Jeremy suggested as he placed his goggles on top of his head. He saw Paul pondering the idea. Jeremy knew he would convince him. The snow was great tonight, packed and soft. Before both went away to school, Gore Mountain used to be their second home. Actually, it was home to several people, being that living in Northern New York didn't give you many options but to enjoy the outdoors. But now, several years later, it was hard to fit in time to talk let alone skiing. He was actually surprised when Paul agreed to go today.

"Okay, one more run, and then we will head in for a beer. Deal?" Paul bargained.

"All right. Meet you at the lift," Jeremy said.

He swooshed down the hill, grazing the edges of the mountain, flirting with the rows of pine trees skirting the trail. He again waited for his friend to catch up with him, and then headed towards the lift. This one would take them to the top of Wild Air, one of the most difficult trails on the mountain. The chair ride would take a while. They waited for the people in front of them to shuffle through the line.

"So, anyway, what's the deal?" Jeremy asked.

"What do you mean, 'what's the deal?'" Paul replied.

"Not only did we find time to ski today but a drink, too? Wow, the local celebrity takes a break," Jeremy joked.

"Okay, smart ass, watch yourself."

The lift neared behind them, and they settled in for the fifteen-minute ride to the top.

Jeremy leaned forward onto the bar and kicked the snow off his skis. "So, anyway, how is work? My mother always says that she sees you reporting. You would not believe how much she raves about it. But seriously, do you like your job?"

"Yeah, I do like it. Actually, it's picking up. I mean, there always has to be news everyday, but now we are starting to work on a series, me and one of the editors."

"Oh, that's cool. That'll look good on a resume. What are you working on?"

"It is really from the result of a tragic event. Did you hear about the Jensen suicide?"

"I did. That was the young girl on the other side of town."

"Well, our news director wants us to do a series on it and maybe some other issues that affect the community. I guess last year another teenager committed suicide. Two within a year and a half is pretty big around here. Even though we can't discuss the facts about that particular case, we can bring the issue into the public eye."

"Yeah, sounds like a good idea. Who are you working on it with?"

"That situation is weird. Her name is Abby Greene. She is the Assignment Editor at the station, but she wants to get into reporting. The strange thing is that we went to talk to Mrs. Jensen, and it was rough."

"The mother was really upset, I guess?"

"Well, yeah, she was upset about her daughter, but it was Abby that found it very troublesome. She didn't know the Jensen girl, but she had a close friend that committed suicide years ago. All of this talk about suicide really got Abby upset. She couldn't even finish the interview. The name doesn't ring a bell, but they are…were, in her friend's case…a few years younger than us. I think Abby said her name was Becca: Becca Parsons. Do you remember her?"

Jeremy couldn't believe what he was hearing. When Paul first started this conversation, he had a disturbing feeling about where it was leading. Jeremy never told anyone about this; he couldn't. Thankfully, the crest of the mountain prevented Jeremy from having to answer. Instead, he grasped the hollow metal bar as they prepared to get off the lift. "Yeah, I don't know," he said, trying to blow off the entire subject. "I'll meet you at the bottom."

With that, he dug his poles into the crisp snow and pushed off as hard as he could. He skied down the hill with reckless abandon. Usually, he took his time, feeling the mountain with all of its grandeur. Now, he was trying to ski away from this awful memory that Paul just invoked. The wind was biting at his face and his eyes streamed with tears, since he hadn't even bothered to pull his goggles down. His heart pounded by the time he raced to the bottom. It wasn't from the exertion; he wished that's all it was. He turned around and waited for Paul. When he noticed that his friend was almost at the bottom, he started to head towards the lodge to lock his skis. He knew the conversation that was going to follow was not going to be easy.

Paul scanned the lodge looking for Jeremy. It wasn't crowded as usual, considering it was the end of the ski day. Like most major resorts, the slopes closed around five. He was actually looking forward to relaxing with one or two beers. He hadn't seen Jeremy in a while and the crazy work schedule didn't leave him much time away from the station. He noticed Jeremy at the table in the back near the enormous stone fireplace. He loved this lodge. It was vast enough to accommodate native as well as vacationing skiers, and there were enough areas that seemed recessed away from screaming kids and rowdy teenagers. He gestured towards the bar before heading to the table and Jeremy gave a nod. He ordered two Heinekens from the bartender then headed to sit down. He relaxed back into the ample, wooden captain's chair and propped his unbuckled boots on the unoccupied one across from him. He slid the beer across the table.

"Heineken, right?" he asked his friend.

"Yeah, that's fine. Probably just one, though, then I have to get going," Jeremy said with a lack of enthusiasm in his voice.

"Come on, I have work, too, but how often do we get to do this? Do you remember when we used to come home from school in the summer? Just one drink was not in our vocabulary." Paul laughed and could tell that Jeremy was not paying attention to him whatsoever. "Hello? Hey, what's going on?" He gave Jeremy a friendly punch to his shoulder.

Jeremy sat hunched over his beer, fumbling with the label. His jet-black hair contrasted greatly against his light skin, but now, even against the warm tones of the fireplace, his complexion looked totally bleak. His normal joking demeanor wasn't present now. His grin was replaced with a tight-lipped grimace.

"You seem out of it," Paul commented. "Are you all right? Sick or something?"

"No, I'm just tired and I have a lot on my mind," Jeremy answered.

"Okay. Did something happen between the top of the mountain and here? You're pissed off about something."

Jeremy took a long gulp from his bottle and pounded it down on the table. "It's nothing, okay? Christ, you don't let up."

A middle-aged couple sitting nearby picked up their drinks and moved across the room to another table. They weren't the only ones that detected anger in Jeremy's voice.

"Hey, listen," Paul said. "I don't know what the hell is going on, but you don't have to act like a total ass."

Jeremy looked into the fire, studying the vibrant orange flames flickering against the mound of wood in the middle. He didn't want to answer Paul. He didn't want to talk about this, but he did know this was going to come up again. How could he think that it wouldn't? Sure, he brought it up to Bob Franklin before, but being a novice in the funeral business he was laughed at and wildly dismissed. The director explained to him that with his first few experiences, he would find himself going above and beyond his job. He'd think he saw something, but it would be just his imagination. In a grotesque kind of way, he would almost want to find something bizarre. Jeremy never wanted to find something like that. Now it had all resurfaced again. Jeremy often thought about it and always questioned himself, but this is the first time he heard someone bring up the subject. It struck a very volatile chord with him. Paul could see that, and now the floodgates were opened. He knew Paul would persevere and get the story out of him.

"I have to tell you something that may sound inconceivable, but I don't know if we should discuss it now," he said. Jeremy watched as Paul's face shifted from anger to an expression of surprise.

Paul looked around, exaggerating that there were not many people surrounding them. "No, come on, whatever it is that's bothering you, tell me. No one is within earshot distance, and neither of us has to be somewhere right now. What's going on?"

Jeremy turned his attention to the condensation-laden bottle. He tried to gather his thoughts, because he knew what Paul was going to ask next. Jeremy questioned the answer to that as well.

"I don't even know where to start," he said. He wiped his hand across his forehead. The coldness from the bottle transferred from his hand to his head. It felt good against his brow. Now if he could just do something about the fire burning in his chest and the sick feeling in his stomach.

Maybe another beer wasn't such a bad idea anyway. "I think I need another one of these first."

Paul hurried to the bar to grab two more drinks and was back before Jeremy could gather his thoughts. Not that he wanted to retrieve them anyway.

Paul plopped back down into the chair. "All right, so what's going on?"

Jeremy sat there for a moment and then figured it was now or never. "Have you ever felt that something wasn't quite right, but just never figured out why?"

"Yeah, I guess. Sometimes that happens with a story I am working on. There have been several murders, kidnappings, and other crimes. The story gets reported and you reveal what you can, but you don't always have all of the answers. It's unsettling, but it happens, and you just deal with it because it is part of the game."

Jeremy realized that Paul wasn't going to understand his story. He figured that he might as well just come right out with it. "Listen, Paul, I have to tell you something that you are going to say sounds farfetched. Today's conversation was too coincidental. You will probably have a million questions, but just hear me out first, okay?"

Paul's carefree look disappeared; his face was now filled with confusion. Jeremy wasn't positive that what he was about to say would change that. Jeremy filled his lungs to a bursting capacity and let out a long sigh, preparing to revisit his nightmare that he kept dormant for too long. Whether it was true or not, it was still his nightmare.

"Well, it's like this: you know how I've always felt about the funeral business; I wanted to be a director since I was a kid. I was thrilled to be helping out at Franklin Funeral Home as a teenager."

Paul gave a weak smile and agreed with him. He listened as Jeremy droned on about having the ability to make people feel at ease and being able to handle such an emotionally demanding profession. Paul always knew that. Jeremy was the only comical, light-hearted, positive funeral director he had ever known…not that he knew many funeral directors.

"Anyway, I have told you many stories before. I have seen some troubling cases," Jeremy continued. "Most of the procedures that people are repulsed to hear about, I can handle. The tough stuff, like picking up bodies, embalming, and preparation, is just work to me. I am able to separate myself from my emotions and do what has to be done. It's my job. But there is something that I still think about from time to time. I still get this uneasy feeling in my stomach when I venture down that path. It resurfaced today. Like I said, call it coincidence or synchronicity, but I took it as a sign that I should tell you."

Paul's expression was of extreme stupor by this point. He could not imagine what his friend was about to say. He wasn't sure he wanted to know.

"I was at Franklin in 1990. Becca Parson's viewing was held there," Jeremy admitted.

"Oh yeah, that's right. It was during the summer when she committed suicide, right?"

"No, you're wrong."

"I could have sworn it was when we were out of school."

"No, I mean you were wrong about Becca committing suicide. I think she was murdered."

Chapter 5

Abby couldn't figure out why she woke during the middle of the night when she had been so tired lately from lack of sleep. She thought about Becca often, but nothing was as intense as the past few days. She couldn't get her out of her mind.

Abby pulled herself out of bed and walked over to her favorite window. She nestled into her precious space and pulled her knees up against her chest. Even though the glass was cold and a slight draft was creeping through one of the faltering moldings, Abby felt safe and enclosed. Her schedule didn't always allow her to sit back and relax. There were days she had to be at the desk very early and her shifts were not consistent. She wasn't considered a full time employee, but she worked enough hours to be close to that.

Abby's goal to be a newscaster started here. She realized that it was a small market and the pay wasn't great, but she was happy to be working in the field. They offered the part time job and she jumped at the chance. She liked the people she worked with and the experience was good. Paying her bills was a little tight some months, but the money set aside for her from her mom helped. If all else failed, her dad would do anything to help her out. But for the most part, Abby tried to be as independent as possible.

Speaking of independent, she was happy to be off of work today. Not being on during the weekend was a rarity. She wanted to straighten up her place, but thought about catching up on her sleep and going back to bed for another hour or so. That idea was changed when she got the call.

"Hey, I didn't wake you up, did I?" Paul asked on the other end.

"No, I'm up. What going on?" She was a little surprised that he was calling. It's not that she didn't get along with Paul, but they were more peers than close friends. Abby figured that their friendly work relationship stayed there.

"Abby, we need to get together today."

"Well, I was supposed to be off, but if you really need something…"

"No, not to come into work; I need you to come over to my place."

Abby was confused and wasn't sure what he needed. "Is this about the Jensen girl again? I was hoping that could wait until next week. Emotionally, I need to take a break from dealing with the situation for a few days," she said with a bit of defense in her voice.

"Can you just come over? It's not about that. I need you to meet someone," he said with no humor in his voice.

"Yeah. Let me get ready. I will be over in about an hour or so. It's Birch Street, right?"

"Yes. You drove by before with me. You know where it is, right?" he asked.

Abby did remember when they were going on a story and he pointed out the old Victorian structure that he rented. The home was divided into four apartments. Abby would die to have one of them.

After hanging up with Paul, she scrambled to get ready. She stared at the two pair of jeans, one pair of khakis, and two black pairs of pants on her bed and decided on her favorite jeans. A charcoal sweater was still appropriate for this time of year, but she hoped that she didn't look too casual. Paul didn't say what was going on, but she was hinging on the fact that they weren't going to go out anywhere. She tried to pull her hair into a high ponytail, then a low one, but finally just brushed it out. The static electricity in the air made her hair out of control, but a few dollops of gel did the trick. She studied her face in the mirror and still couldn't figure out why most people said she had good cheekbones. She thought her face looked sunken in, but her complexion was youthful. She attributed her clear skin to her mother. She tried to not overdo it with makeup, just a little mascara and blush followed by her favorite tinted lip-gloss. Her black boots were under the table in the living room and she groaned when she leaned over to get them. She was going to wait until the spring to start running again, but her jeans were telling her differently.

She ran into the bedroom contemplating the several articles of clothing strewn on her down comforter, but after glancing at the clock, decided there was no time to change. Instead, she grabbed a bagel and headed out the door.

* * * *

Abby pulled up in front of Paul's apartment. She pulled down her visor and squinted at the reflection in the mirror. Her flawless skin looked so pale and washed out today. Maybe skipping the heavy makeup wasn't such a good idea. Paul saw her every day; she wasn't sure what she was worrying about. She wasn't sure who else was meeting them there. She realized that no matter how much she ran her fingers through her hair, it was going to look the same.

She stepped onto the front porch and studied the mailboxes. They were made out of beautiful, antique brass. Abby liked the look of Paul's place and she wasn't even through his threshold. As she was about to try the glass handle that led to the hallway, the door swung open.

"Hey, Abby, how are you doing? Come in. I'll give you the grand tour, if that's what you want to call it."

Paul was dressed in jeans and a black turtleneck. He wore suede moccasins with no socks. Abby thought it looked kind of cute.

Paul must have caught her staring. "You like my shoes, don't you?" he asked, wiggling the leather-covered foot in front of her.

She laughed and followed him into his living room. Paul led her over to meet a man standing across the room. He was shorter than Paul and had jet-black hair. He seemed nervous and fidgety as Paul introduced him. He extended his hand and pumped Abby's with a strong handshake. She always took notice of that in people. Her father always said you could judge someone by their handshake.

"Hi, Jeremy Greish. It's nice to meet you, Abby," he said.

"Hi, nice to meet you," she replied. She had no idea who he was but he looked familiar. She tried to break the ice by commenting on Paul's apartment.

"This is really nice, Paul," she said, looking around. There was a fireplace in the living room with ornate carvings within the moldings encasing it. An enormous mirror sat directly above the hearth. The corners had a faded black speckling that revealed its age. Paul didn't do much in the line of interior decorating, but the structure spoke for itself. It didn't need much help.

"Yeah, I guess it's pretty nice. I didn't need something like this, but I couldn't pass up the good deal on it. My parents knew the owner, so it worked out. Let me show you the kitchen," he offered.

Jeremy stayed in the living room and stared mindlessly at the television. He heard Paul mention something about how he didn't even pay much attention to the black marble counter. It was evident that Abby was impressed with the apartment. Who wouldn't be? Everything always seemed to work out for Paul. Jeremy realized that Abby continued to peer into the living room. Her glare was directed at him, but when she caught him staring back, she diverted her attention, pretending to be interested in Paul's fireplace hearth in the kitchen. Jeremy knew that she recognized him. She had to. He was surprised that she didn't notice at first, but it was inevitable that she would put two and two together. Jeremy swallowed hard but was unsuccessful in clearing the lump that he felt in his throat. He picked up a newspaper and tried to look engrossed in the front page as the two returned to the room.

"Can I get the two of you something to drink?" Paul asked.

Abby wanted water; Jeremy, nothing.

As Paul walked back into the kitchen, Abby and Jeremy were faced with a few moments alone. The two of them awaited Paul's return with great anticipation.

"So, Jeremy, where do I know you from? Are you from the area?" she asked.

Jeremy knew what was coming. It would all piece together for her soon enough. He humored her. "Actually, yes, I am. I used to go to high school here and work part time. After college, I moved back to work here again."

"Same here. I moved away to school and then back to Watertown and landed the job at WWNY. You know, you look so familiar, but I still can't place you. You graduated with Paul, right?" she asked.

"I did. We probably know each other from school, even though we didn't hang around together. You know how it is in high school with even a few years difference."

Abby knew exactly what he meant. She knew that Paul went to the same high school, and she vaguely remembered Jeremy, but both would have been a few years older than her. Not by much, but the difference between a freshman and senior is huge. "And you're working in the area now, here in Watertown?" Abby asked.

Jeremy strained to look for Paul. He didn't want to start this without him. He wasn't sure how to lead into his explanation.

Paul walked in at the right moment and sat on the ottoman across the room from Abby.

"Paul, Abby was just asking me about where I work," he informed his friend.

This prompted Paul to move to the edge of his seat with his hands clasped under his chin. He looked up at Jeremy and acknowledged that he knew it was time to talk.

"I, um, work in town…at Franklin," he said.

"Franklin, as in Franklin Funeral Home?" Abby asked. Her friendly small talk voice changed to something that reflected her annoyance.

"Yes, that's it. I used to help out there part-time when I was younger. I went away to mortuary school and then decided to come back. I have several ties here, you know."

"Yeah, I know," she said as she shifted in her seat. She realized now what was going on. This was somehow related to the Jensen suicide and the series. It annoyed her that after she expressed to Paul that she needed to get away from everything for a few days, he rolled forward with persistence and no concern. "Look, guys, if we are going to start talking about the Jensens or the series or anything like that, maybe the two of you can talk, but I will have to chat some other time." She grabbed her purse and walked over to the archway.

"Abby, Jeremy knows everything about Becca. More than you know. I think you should stay. You may not want to hear this, but you need to know what is going on," Paul quickly said.

Abby spun around and glared at Paul. Jeremy was busy staring at his hands, trying hard to avoid her. She wasn't sure what this was about. She sat back down on the chair, perched on its edge. She listened and waited with great anxiety to hear what this stranger could possibly know about her best friend, Becca.

Jeremy put his glass down on the end table. He wanted to make this explanation as simple as possible, but it was far from uncomplicated. "Abby, I want to cut to the chase. I've worked at Franklin for many years. When I first became interested in that area of work, I was a teenager. My family didn't live too far from Bob Franklin, and when I asked, he gave me a job helping out around the funeral home. I would assist with maintenance, lawn care, and then started to learn more about the business itself. I was working there when Becca died. Mr. Franklin didn't even want me to see the body; he didn't think I could handle it since she was so young."

He paused and studied Abby's face to see if he should proceed with his story. She had a stare locked on him that wouldn't allow him to do anything else but continue. "Anyway, as I got more experience working there, he started to let me observe the embalming process and learn how to plan services. He didn't want me to have to be troubled by Becca's death, but I have to admit, I was curious."

Abby shifted in her seat and placed her hands underneath her. She responded to Jeremy with an over-exaggerated sigh. She didn't want to hear this. "Curious? That's nice."

"No, no, no, I didn't mean that. I didn't know Becca, and I just didn't understand how a girl so young could die. It did bother me, but I felt that if I saw the body, it would make some sort of sense," Jeremy explained. Abby's stare continued to pierce him as he proceeded with his story. "There is a separate structure in the back of the home where we do our embalming. One night after school, I stopped by the funeral home to talk to Mr. Franklin. There was no one in the house, so I made my way to the back. When I walked in, I interrupted him during the embalming process."

"On Becca," Abby responded with coldness in her voice.

"Yes, on Becca. As soon as he heard the door open and saw that it was me, he suggested that I should leave. He went into the same song and dance about it being too disturbing and that my parents probably wouldn't appreciate it. I explained to him that it wouldn't bother me. He said nothing and returned to the table. I approached with caution and saw her small body on the table. Mr. Franklin stepped back for a moment and we both stood there for a few wordless moments. He apologized for snapping at me but wanted me to know that young cases like this still bother him every time, and it never gets any easier. He put his arm around me and patted my shoulder. It was very upsetting. This pitiful sight made me think that the person lying in front of me was only a few years younger. That's when I noticed it." He stopped and tried to force himself to go on with the details of what he saw.

"You noticed what, Jeremy? What?" Abby exclaimed.

Paul looked over at her and knew that she was not going to last much longer discussing funerals and her friend's death. He would finish the story if he had to. "Jer, just tell her already," he said to his friend.

"Before I left the embalming room, I noticed a few scratches and bruises on her body. Her hand that was peeking out from underneath the sheet also revealed a few cuts and scrapes. I asked Mr. Franklin about it and wondered why there were all of those injuries if she overdosed on pills. He explained to me that maybe she fell after being overcome by the strong effects of the pills."

Abby took a few minutes to gather her thoughts. "Can I ask what the hell you are getting at?"

This was the part he had to try to just say and not explain. He couldn't explain it to himself. He couldn't fully explain it to Paul. He surely couldn't explain it to Abby. "Abby, I have to tell you I have always had a bad feeling about the situation. After seeing Becca's body, I doubted over and over again in my mind the issue of how she died. Mr. Franklin's answer about the scratches didn't make much sense, either."

"So you think she died another way?" Abby asked.

"I do. But I don't think it was by her own hand either."

"What Jeremy is saying is that he thinks there may be reason to believe that foul play was involved in Becca's death," Paul summarized.

Abby tapped her foot on the floor for a few seconds while Paul and Jeremy waited with great patience for some sort of response. She jumped out of her chair and turned her attention to Jeremy. "So let's see. A teenager gets the thrill of his life by helping out at a funeral home. Why, I don't know, but nevertheless, you had this vision of a dream job. So then, your imagination goes wild and you think you are a big shot investigator with all of the answers. Believe me, I try every day to think of why she would have killed herself, but I don't find the answers by blaming someone with murder. Are you out of your mind? What the hell kind of theory is that? Don't you think someone would have caught on to something like that? The police? Mr. Franklin? The Rices? Why would someone murder a twelve-year-old girl? No, you know what: I'm not even going to ask any more questions. It's been many years and people suffered enough. Why you have to bring this up now I'll never know." She geared her anger towards Paul. "Oh, maybe it's for the suicide series, right, Paul? Maybe this could be Paul's big break and big story," she said, throwing her hands up in front of her. She grabbed her purse and headed for the door.

"Abby, wait, I still want to explain. All of these years I had this lingering suspicion that something wasn't right, but I couldn't do anything about it. When Paul mentioned the series and your name and then Becca's, I just thought it was fate and that I had to say something. I took it as a sign," Jeremy pleaded.

Abby glared with fire in her eyes at both of them. "Well, nice try. It makes for a great news story, but personally, I think you are both self-centered. I am going." She walked out the door and ran down the steps, digging in her purse for her keys. She started crying and couldn't stop.

"Hey, need these?" Paul asked, dangling the silver keychain in front of her. He lowered his voice so many octaves that Abby could barely hear him. "Hey, why don't you come back inside? Jeremy didn't mean to upset you. He just thought you should know. It's probably all so farfetched, but he needed to tell you. I am sorry, Abby. We didn't mean to rattle you." His eyes were sincere and he looked just as troubled as she. He bit his bottom lip waiting for any response from Abby.

"It's just in the past few days, all of these feelings about her were dredged up and I can't deal with it," she said.

She started sobbing again and Paul embraced her with a strong hug. He held her shoulders and looked her in the eyes.

"Listen, why don't you go home and we could talk about this tomorrow. I'll drive you back if you want, okay?"

Abby contemplated the idea but decided to go back into his apartment. Now that the initial gush of emotions had passed, she was curious to see what else Jeremy had to say. At least she thought so.

She didn't say anything to Paul as they walked back onto the porch, especially the fact that she was upset for the most part because all of her emotions and bad memories were stirred up. She didn't mention that she shared some of the same views and ideas that Jeremy did. That scared her the most.

Chapter 6

Jonathan Rice and his wife, Theresa, lived on beautiful Indian Lake. The home they lived in was similar to many others in the area, but had many unique qualities. Their Victorian structure exuded an intriguing personality. It had a typical rounded turret as expected from such a house, but there wasn't a grand wrap around porch sprawling from front to back. Tucked away, starting from a back corner, was a peaceful side patio that extended around the back of the structure. The ivy-laden trellis hid major columns and support beams. There were no neighbors for at least two miles. The isolation added to the splendid solitude experienced here.

Theresa gathered her work from the dining room table. The gleaming, deep mahogany surface extended eight place-settings long. This room was a splendid combination of darkness and light. The moldings that encased each doorway and window were carved with great detail. The deep shades of its wooden composure matched its furniture counterpart. The three stained glass windows depicting scenes of progression from day to night allowed colorful light to splash off of the glossy surfaces within the room. The first window allowed light to pass through its vibrant glass, permitting its own picture of the sun to cast golden hues wherever the filtered beam fell. Theresa's hand was illuminated as she passed her sleeve over a small smudge that crossed into the streaming brilliance. Her heels pierced the silence of the room as she walked across the hardwood.

"Jonathan, do you want to go out? All of this work has me exhausted. I couldn't even begin to think of what to make for dinner," Theresa called into the other room.

"Sure, that's fine. Hey, before you go upstairs, can you see if someone is here? I thought I heard a car," Jonathan said from behind his newspaper.

It was still winter in Watertown and although the Lake George region attracted many skiers and snowmobile riders, the big season was months away. Many tourists would comb the area for places to stay. On several occasions, the Rices would receive a knock at their door, someone inquiring about a room, thinking their home was a bed and breakfast. The two had considered this before, but their obsession for the home kept them as the sole residents year round.

Theresa pushed the ivory lace curtain that was attached both at the top and bottom of the etched glass on the door to see who arrived. "Do you know someone that drives a green Honda?" she asked, resting the tip of her nose against the glass.

"Not that I know of. Probably just someone looking to stay here," he said, without even glancing towards the door.

Theresa held her hand on the cool brass doorknob waiting for their visitor. She surprised the young woman with an instantaneous response to her knock.

The heavy oak door opened and Abby dropped one of her blue-lined tablets out of her bag. She scrambled to pick it up. This wasn't going as smoothly as she hoped.

"Hi, there. Sorry," Abby said. She waited to see an expression of surprise on Theresa's face. It was obvious that the woman didn't recognize her. She managed a weak smile. She stepped back and allowed Abby to walk into the foyer.

"Can I help you with something?" Theresa asked, humoring Abby like she was a passing tourist.

Abby had hoped Theresa would find something vaguely familiar about her. Her hairstyle had changed from when she was young. It was always long, but worn pulled off of her face into a high ponytail. She could remember tugging and pulling her mane trying to smooth it and secure it with a small elastic band. People's facial features change, but there is always a distinct feature that makes each person different. With Abby, it was her nose. She felt that the small bump right near the bridge looked out of place on her face, making her nose look too big. Her mother always said it gave her character and that not everyone can have perfect features. On the other hand, she inherited her mom's prominent cheekbones. They weren't severe, as most people would desire, but rather implied softness with great definition. Abby had pictures of herself and her mother grinning from ear to ear. The defined, rosy facial expressions were an immediate give-away that they were mother and daughter. She thought often how much she missed that smile.

"You probably don't remember me. It's been years," she stammered. Everything that Abby planned on saying was coming out all wrong. Her nerves took over her mouth and ran with it. "I'm Abby, Abby Greene. Becca and I used to be friends," she said as her voice went up a few octaves. As she mouthed the words, she realized how ridiculous she sounded. "I, well, I was wondering if I could…" She trailed off as Jonathan appeared in the archway.

"Oh my God, Abby," he said, barely above a whisper.

She was happy that he ended her torment and embarrassment of this failing introduction. Jonathan stood there motionless. It had been over a decade, but he hadn't changed much. The dark hair that Abby remembered looked like it started to turn gray. He had on a navy turtleneck and jeans. The chiseled facial features started to give way to clusters of wrinkles around the corner of each eye. His skin was a bit dark for this time of year, which Abby figured was from a recent vacation. Jonathan looked over the top of his small, black-rimmed glasses. As he watched Abby, she also realized that his athletic build that she remembered was still ever present, just a little softer now. The signs of middle age settled on Jonathan with grace. She wasn't sure who should speak next. The inevitable would come up sooner or later, and that's the discussion Abby feared most.

"It's been many years, Abby," he said. "How are you? What have you been up to? Well, wait, please come in first." He gestured for her to settle in the living room.

Abby glanced around at everything that was situated just as she remembered. There was some remodeling that had been done, and the furnishing was different, but for the most part, it brought back memories. Jonathan must have sensed her feelings right away.

"It brings back several happy thoughts," he said, gazing around the room. "I know you and Becca played together all of the time when she lived here. She really adored you."

An uncomfortable silence followed. Neither of them wanted to bring up Becca first. She was glad that he did.

"Oh, I'm sorry, you remember my wife Theresa, don't you?" he asked.

"I do. It's nice to see you, Theresa," she said, acknowledging her with a smile.

"Same here. I'm sorry I didn't recognize you right away. Boy, have you grown up. You look great." Theresa stared at Abby wide-eyed.

While she was sitting there reminiscing about the good times from her childhood, Abby realized that they didn't ask why she was there. She was getting sicker by the minute knowing why she came and what she needed to discuss. Abby thought that maybe it was just best to leave and explain her ludicrous story another day. An explanation was needed as to why she was in this area. It's wasn't a home she passed every day. It didn't make sense to drop in on them after no communication for twelve years. She didn't have to initiate that part of the conversation, but she still had to explain it. However, she was so afraid of upsetting them and stirring up bad memories after talking about all of the cherished ones.

"So, what brings you here anyway, Abby?" Jonathan asked.

"Well, I have been working at WWNY for over a year now. I've been doing assignment editor work, nothing on air yet. That's what I am eventually striving for."

"That great, Abby, really it is. So, is there some big story around here that you were in the area for?" Theresa asked, leaning onto her hands that were placed on her knees.

"No, actually the reason I am here is to ask you a few questions. We are doing a series at work on teen suicide," Abby said. She watched as Jonathan shifted in his chair, averting Abby's eyes. She knew this would be difficult. "It's hard, but I am trying to relate some of the current situations to Becca's case. I am having a tough time with it, but I am working with a great reporter who is helping me through it. We feel that if we can prevent someone else from ending his or her life, then our efforts will be worthwhile." She studied both of their faces for some kind of feedback and to see where she should go from there. She couldn't do it. She couldn't bring up the question about murder. She felt like she would be putting too much pain and pressure on him to think of such a horrid thought.

Jonathan rubbed the heels of his hands into his thighs and sighed. "Wow, Abby. It's been so long, but yet I can still remember everything like it was just yesterday. We would be glad to help you as much as we can, but as I am sure you can relate to, all of that digging brings up some difficult memories to digest."

"No, that's fine. And please tell me if you think that you can't do this. If it is too hard, then we will just forget the question and answer session. I felt that I could talk to you more easily about it. We both went through a tough time," she said.

That was it for today. There was no way that she could continue with the new theory proposed by Jeremy. The Rices were visibly shaken. There was no way she could unload information such as that on them. She was still having a hard time dealing with the thought of it, but it would have to come out sooner or later. Sooner was not the right time, and Abby respected that. Her anticipation and curiosity were quelled by the look of sadness on their faces. Her questions would wait. She stood up and hinted that she should leave. The Rices jumped on the invitation.

"We agree. We would like to help prevent something so tragic affecting anyone else's family. Although Becca didn't stay with us very long, we loved taking her in as our own child. She was a welcomed addition to our home, giving us great joy and happiness. We were going to move after it happened, but decided to do extensive remodeling instead. Becca loved this house and we think she would have wanted us to stay and keep it in the family. We miss her dearly," Jonathan said, putting his arm around his wife.

"I know it must be hard for you. There is not a day that goes by that I don't miss her. But, anyway, thank you, Jonathan, Theresa. Thanks for talking, and I guess I will be in touch soon. Take care and remember, if this is too difficult, I'll understand," she said.

"Thanks, Abby. We will see you soon," Jonathan said as he walked her to the door and onto the porch.

Abby headed to her car and pulled her collar around her neck. The temperature must have plummeted ten degrees since she first arrived. She turned around to wave one last time and noticed that Jonathan and Theresa looked upset. It looked like they were arguing. They paused when they noticed Abby not in her car yet, smiled, waved, and closed the door. Abby knew this topic would upset them. She couldn't even imagine how distraught they would be if she ever brought up the subject of murder.

Abby revved the engine on the Honda a few times and thought it would escalate the heat. Her frosty breath and shivering hands proved otherwise. The carpets were perpetually damp from getting in and out with snow or slush on her boots. It produced a musty, damp smell that she couldn't get rid of. It was still present, but mixed with the strawberries and cream air freshener that dangled from her mirror.

As she drove down the driveway, two deer darted across the road. She slammed on the breaks but thankfully wasn't going very fast. The two graceful creatures paraded across the narrow pathway. They stopped and stared at Abby's car. She leaned against the steering wheel and watched them as they pranced back into the woods. They were so unassuming without any cares. She wished she felt that way.

Chapter 7

The newsroom at WWNY was peaceful today. Abby liked working the weekends. Even though it was a skeleton crew manning the shift, it allowed her to be more versatile and multifaceted with her day-to-day duties. Her weekend work gave her the best experience.

She needed to talk to Paul to get his view on things, but he was currently out covering the fire that gutted a home not too far from the station. The element of disappointment was sure to hang in the air once he realized that she didn't go through with all of her questions. She couldn't. It was hard enough to approach the house, let alone bring up the notion that a murder could have been committed.

Ever since she barked at Jeremy when he explained his theory, she couldn't get it out of her mind. She didn't want him to know that he wasn't the first to ponder the situation. It happened several times, closer to when Becca died. There were many nights that Abby would lie in her bed in the days following the funeral in an entranced state. She wanted to be in Becca's mind and figure out what she was thinking. She played the situation over and over again in her head. Abby didn't deny the fact that Becca had to endure hardships: the loss of her mother was devastating, not to mention that she had to experience the tragedy at such a young age. Abby was older when she lost her mother, but it was still a very painful experience. It must have been difficult to have to go through something so trying. However, Becca talked about her feelings. She mentioned her mom often and tried to tell Abby about all the good times. Becca resented her father for abandoning them, but she never said she hated him. Abby always thought that at least she had Jonathan and Theresa.

Abby knew that even though she had a short-term friendship with Becca, she knew her well. Becca was a young girl with dreams and aspirations. She could use the hardship in her life to turn things around and make something of herself. They were only twelve years old, but Becca talked about school in the future. She wanted to be a doctor, then a painter, then a musician. Her dreams changed from day to day, but they existed. Sure, Becca was a soft-spoken, shy girl, but she did not act depressed. Abby could not imagine how Becca could take her own life; she wouldn't hurt herself, but mainly, she wouldn't do something like that to hurt others. There may have not been many people close to her in her life, but Abby didn't think Becca would hurt her best friend.

The only problem was, if she didn't kill herself, why would anyone want to? That made Abby uneasy. It was unlikely that her death was anything but a suicide. If that was the case, Becca did hurt the one that loved her. This was an issue that haunted Abby for years. She had an unsettling feeling and knew that either answer had one outcome: Becca was never coming back. But could she have prevented it? That may be something she would have to live with and question forever. It was the other thing she resented. She wasn't sure what she wanted to hear. The fact that Jeremy appeared in her life was not just coincidence. Abby didn't believe in coincidence, only synchronicity.

Her thoughts were halted by the sound of someone walking down the hall. She assumed and hoped that it was Paul. As the footsteps grew closer, she recognized the sound of his rubber-soled loafers with his quickened pace. He rounded the corner and smiled as soon as he saw Abby. She wasn't used to having someone so happy to see her besides her dad, but she was also sure that Paul was eager to get the story from her as to what happened at the Rices'.

"Well, how did it go?" he asked with enthusiasm.

Abby hushed him and gave him a frown, nodding towards one of the small edit bays. There were very few people that worked on Saturday, but Paul's camera man was already busy editing the story they just shot.

Paul waved his hands towards the camera man. "Don't worry about him," he whispered as he pulled a chair in front of Abby's desk. "So tell me: how surprised were they?"

"By what?" Abby played dumb.

"The theory? Your entire purpose for going over there? You did bring it up, didn't you?" The silence instead of a response was not what he anticipated. "You didn't bring it up. Abby," he whined. "I told you I would have come with you if you needed help."

Abby did not like the boastful Paul that was surfacing. She knew she could handle it herself, but didn't feel that it was the time. Her personal connections hindered her. "I'm sorry if I couldn't sit down and chat about Becca like it was the latest gossip in Watertown. I plan on going back to talk to them. I'm not totally unsure as to what I am doing," she said.

"I didn't mean that you didn't, Abby. I just know that you want to find out the answers, and if you need help, I am here."

Abby looked at his face and could tell that he was wincing, waiting for another blow from her. Instead, she apologized. "I didn't mean to snap and I know that you are trying to help. This is hard for me, but I am not saying that I don't want to do it. I am trying to be professional here, and it's just taking me a little time to get things straightened out. Why don't we just talk about this later?" she suggested, trying to change the subject.

Paul leaned in closer as if now he didn't want anyone to hear him. "Whatever you want to do. And if you don't want me to go with you, that's fine, too. But we can talk about that later. Do you want to grab something to eat after work?"

"Sure, but later. I was going to stay late tonight. I already said I would work a few hours into the next shift. If you want to come back…and then if it's not too late," she said, making excuses.

"It won't be too late. I'll meet you at Mill Break when you are finished. Call me," he said. He flashed his unforgiving smile and sat down at his desk.

The rest of the day Abby was busy. She did the voiceover for a piece that the new guy shot with Paul, but it was Abby's voice nonetheless. By the time ten-thirty rolled around, she was tired. The thought of going over to Mill Break after working an extra shift made her yawn, but the promise made to Paul would not allow an early return home. Abby searched through her bag for the number that she scrawled on the border of her tablet from earlier in the day. The phone rang a few times. Abby figured he was out already, since it was a Saturday. Just as she was about to hang up, Paul answered the phone.

"Oh, hi. It's me. I was just wondering if you wanted to take a rain check on that drink at Mill Break. I'm pretty beat," she said. She wanted to see him and spill some more of her emotions on the table, but she knew it was going to be an involved process. They were just as well doing it another night.

"How about just one? It's Saturday night. It's too early to go home, Abby. Live a little," Paul said, surprising her as well as annoying her.

She figured she would have to meet him now.

"I will head over there soon. Just one, that's it," she said while Paul laughed. "I'll see you there."

One of the other anchors, Rich, was still in the newsroom. He yelled over to Abby, "So you're going out with Pauly tonight?"

Rich was one of WWNY's newest anchors and did not fit in at the station. His slightly bronzed skin looked more in place somewhere in West Palm Beach than Watertown, but everyone had his or her own look.

Second of all, he didn't know Abby well enough, or Paul for that matter, to be joking around and saying *Pauly*.

She decided to just shrug it off. "We are not going out. I told him I would stop by to get something to eat, that's all."

"Sounds like a date to me," Rich said in a singsong voice.

His childish behavior and better-than-everyone attitude made Abby hope he would transfer to a bigger market sooner than later.

"No, Rich, it's not. You're welcome to stop over if you want," she offered. The reason she freely extended the invitation was because she knew he would never pass up an opportunity to be with one of the three different girls he was dating, but she didn't want him to get the impression that she and Paul were dating. That was all she needed going through the office.

"Sorry, dear, I already have big plans," he said, kicking his feet up on the desk.

"I'm sure you do," Abby muttered under her breath. She gathered her things and walked towards the door. "Goodnight, Rich," she said in her most forced polite voice.

"Goodnight, hon; have fun," he said, trailing off in that nursery rhyme tone again.

Abby rolled her eyes and pushed through the door. She readied her keys before arriving in front of her car. The dark parking lot always made her nervous, but she would rather risk the walk than to ask Rich to escort her outside.

By the time she made it to Mill Break, it was crowded. The flickering Rolling Rock sign in the window was an indication that they were open, as if one couldn't tell from the parking situation. She found a spot close to the building, and managed to squeeze in between a beat up pickup and a large, old Cadillac. Mill Break Pub was definitely one of the hot spots, one of the only bars this close to both work and home. The bonus was that they served food late into the evening. On some nights, they had live music. Abby hoped that tonight wasn't one of those nights. Her re-occurring headache was just starting to twinge in her upper left temple. As she got closer to the door, she only heard the hustle and bustle from the patrons inside, plus the background of the jukebox. She could deal with that.

She walked in, and the door announced her entrance by an annoying, grating sound. Several heads at the bar turned to look at the newest addition to Mill Break's Saturday night party.

The place wasn't very big. The actual bar was in a room in the back. The two connecting rooms contained tables, with one room also housing the pool table and dartboard. Through the haze of smoke, she strained her eyes, looking for Paul. If she didn't see him in the next second, she planned on just turning around. Unfortunately, she saw his outstretched hand flagging her down at the back of the room. There was no going home now.

"It took you long enough. What do you want?" he asked, making Abby's drink preference a priority in their conversation. Paul's rosy glow and glossy eyes led her to believe that he headed over here as soon as he got off the phone earlier.

"A decent microbrew would be great, thanks. Something from Breaker Brewing. As for being late, I got cornered by our friend Rich at the station, so I couldn't leave right away."

"Cornered? What do you mean *cornered?*" Paul yelled over the music.

"You know what I mean. He started talking about his Saturday night adventures, and I couldn't escape the stories," she lied. She didn't want to bring up the comments he made about her and Paul being on a date. It wasn't an extreme, off-the-wall idea but not something that would be entertained.

Abby wasn't hungry before, but Mill Break's famous wings always pulled her in. She promised for the New Year that she would stay away, but it was almost impossible to deny yourself the best chicken wings in New York State.

The waitress looked tired but sounded pleasant as she approached the table. Abby didn't recognize her. She disappeared and materialized with her draft before Abby could decide if she wanted the hot, hickory, or general alarm wing sauce. As the waitress placed her beer on the napkin in front of her, the near overfill of the liquid prompted Abby to pick up the heavy glass and take in the foam before it spilled. The amber ale tasted good as she sipped from the glass. She didn't drink often, but when she did, she enjoyed a quality beer. Abby slipped off her coat and pushed it to the side of the booth. She was glad she came out after all.

"See, wings and beer; the entire night wasn't a flop, right?" Paul smiled.

Abby wondered if he was sitting here drinking for an hour by himself. It was obvious that he had a few, but she doubted that he was alone. He had that type of personality that drew people to him. He would always keep the conversation going. Paul was never at a loss for words.

Just as she suspected, a man with a blue and black flannel coat and nylon webbed cap nodded towards Paul and lifted his beer towards him. He looked down in front of him and realized that the waitress left a small shot glass in front of him. "Thanks, bud," Paul yelled to the man.

"Now who was that?" Abby laughed. "Sometimes I think you know everyone,"

"That was just a guy I was talking to while waiting."

"I figured as much." Abby shifted in the vinyl seat and caught the hem of her sweater on something. She reached down and felt a giant tear in the seat, overflowing with foam. Abby thought to herself that at least the company was good and the beer flowing. She laughed out loud and moved over a few inches.

"What's so funny?" Paul asked.

"Nothing; it's just this place, that's all. Anyway, so when do you want to go to the Rices' with me?" she asked. She figured she wouldn't argue with him about whether or not they would go together; she would just tell him they would. It would make things easier. Paul would help guide the conversation, even though she was more involved in the entire situation. The main problem Abby had was bringing up the issue of murder. She wasn't sure how often the Rices thought about their niece. It could still be hard for them twelve years later, but from the conversation she had, they seemed like they were doing okay, for the most part. She had a feeling that they wouldn't be at such ease after she brought up her ideas. *Murder.* Every time she thought about that, the idea got more and more ridiculous. She would deem it as downright insane if she didn't have the same feeling as Jeremy did nestled all the way in the back of her mind.

Before Paul could question her or refuse her invitation, two-dozen pungent wings with a side of bleu cheese and celery were placed in front of Abby. She was sure that these diet killers were a mistake. Paul reached over for a napkin and a drumstick.

"Thanks. I was thinking that we could go tomorrow, if you'd like. You're doing the early, right?" he asked.

"Yep," she said, in between pauses from licking her fingers. She wasn't sure if Paul thought that was inappropriate, but he didn't seem to mind or even notice. The orange sauce on the corner of his mouth tarnished an otherwise beautiful smile. His teeth showed signs of being perfected by braces at an early age. His smile was attention getting, but his devilish smirk was just as enticing. Abby wasn't the only one who realized she was staring.

"What's wrong?" he asked.

Trying not to embarrass him, she took a drink from her glass and then motioned to the side of her mouth with her napkin.

"Oh, thanks," he said. "We can go right after work if you want to. Call them tomorrow morning and make sure it's okay."

"I will, but I am sure it will be fine," she said. "I'll really have to get home soon. It's going to be a long day."

"Ahh, have another beer; you'll be fine. So tell me, how do you think Mr. and Mrs. Rice will respond to your theory? Do you think they ever entertained the idea that you are proposing?" he asked.

Abby really didn't think they were going to want to hear it, let alone ever thought about it. Plus, they would want to know who she thought could have committed such a crime and why. Abby didn't have to think too hard until someone popped into her mind. And if that was the case, more people than not would be very disturbed by her answer.

"I don't know what they are going to say, but I am sure they will be upset. Let's talk about it tomorrow. I really have to get going after this," she said, pointing to her plate.

Paul reached over and grabbed two wings, and Abby managed to finish her beer with ease. She figured she deserved one more before she went, but knew she would need a hell of a lot more to calm herself for tomorrow's talk with the Rices.

Chapter 8

The following workday went by slowly. The newsroom was buzzing as usual, but every time Abby looked at the clock, it seemed to have only moved a few minutes. Her mind wasn't on what she was doing. She kept going over what she needed to say to the Rices and how she would respond to their reaction. She just wanted to get this out there. The anticipation of telling them made her stomach do flip-flops.

Paul walked by her desk and stopped to give her a quizzical glare. He leaned over her desk. "What are you doing? Are you okay?" he asked.

It was obvious that he noticed Abby's labored and exaggerated breathing. She was certain that he thought she was a strange one for sure.

"Deep breathing helps me relax," she explained. "I guess I am nervous about this entire thing. I'll be okay."

Paul muttered something about needing another beer to do the trick and walked away. At least someone found humor in this day. She felt very warm and wondered if she should have worn something different. Her gray cowl neck sweater was suffocating her, but she liked how it looked with her black pants. There weren't many things in her wardrobe that she could say she loved, so when she found something that did a fairly good job in complementing her, she would wear it to feel more confident. Abby resigned herself to the fact that she would never be extremely thin, but she was always working to lose an extra ten pounds. Everyone said her five foot five inch frame looked fine, but she always thought otherwise.

The short hall next to the newsroom led to the dressing room for the news anchors, but the area looked more like a glorified closet than prep room. Across the drab, tan wall stretched a mirror and a long shelf. Several bottles of hairspray, makeup, and creams cluttered the counter. Abby used one of the blotting papers and studied her reflection in the mirror. The single glaring fluorescent light bar above did not do much for her complexion. She pulled her hair away from her face and studied her profile. She had talked about getting a shorter cut, but knew she didn't have the courage to do so. She let her dark tresses fall back down, grazing her shoulders.

Abby started to head back to her desk to call Jonathan. As she walked to the door, a reporter that was out all day plopped on the small stool placed in front of the mirror.

The petite brunette sighed as she wiped away at her smudged charcoal eyeliner.

"Hi, Abby," she said. "God, what a day. Look at me; I look terrible."

Yeah, terrible, Abby thought. *She was probably out all day in the wind and running from place to place and she still looks flawless.* Nonetheless, she reassured the near-perfect woman that she looked fine, but rolled her eyes as she walked out, reminded of the fact that vanity was just as important as skill.

Abby called the Rice house again and got the answering machine. She left a message saying that unless she hears from them, she and Paul would be stopping over after work.

Around six-thirty p.m. she sauntered over to Paul's desk.

"One second and I will be finished. I just have to make two more phone calls and then we can go," he said as he turned his focus from his computer to the phone.

Abby went back to the desk and started putting her things away. She wasted some time by rummaging through her bag, looking for items to organize. There were some things in her life that she couldn't control, but throwing out old papers kept her feeling somewhat organized. She discovered the reason why her bag was so heavy. Magazines poured out that were marked with paper clips. She knew they were saved for a reason, but couldn't remember why. An assignment editor always looked for stories and information. Whenever she would see something good, she would save it. Abby settled on rearranging what junk she had and slid it back with some order into her black bag.

The smell of burnt coffee wafted into the room. Someone either left the pot on or was gearing up for a long night. She hoped Paul would hurry so they could get over there and complete their task. Finally, he grabbed his bag and held the door for her as they headed outside.

"Do you mind if I drive?" Paul asked and stopped before walking toward his car.

Abby didn't mind in the least. She loved her green machine, but it wasn't the most presentable car to cart others around in. "No, that's fine," she said, walking towards his sedan.

The black car fit Paul's personality. It still said young but was sophisticated enough to show his maturity.

"So what should I expect from Jonathan and Theresa Rice?" he asked as he drove.

"I don't know. I knew them for that one summer when Becca lived there and I didn't keep in touch with them after her death. They're nice. Just your average people, I guess. I'm not sure why they never had children. I think it might have something to do with the guilt after losing Becca."

"What do you mean by *guilt?*"

"Well, Becca's mom trusted them to take care of something precious to her after she was gone, and Jonathan probably felt like he let his sister down. I mean, I don't know for sure, but that's what I would think. When I was over there the other day, they were willing to talk about it but not at great lengths. It's not their fault that Becca committed suicide, but I'm sure they wonder what they could have done to prevent it. I know I do."

"Ab, I'm sorry. I keep forgetting your role in this. If you're not okay with anything, let me know."

Abby wasn't sure how she felt. As far as she was concerned, the book on this topic was open now, and she couldn't let it shut until she had some answers, although it pained her to have to re-live the sorrow and grief associated with the memory of Becca. It bothered her that they would resurrect these difficult feelings for everyone. She knew that if there was something more to this story, it had to be revealed. Somewhere in her realm of thinking, Abby had to remember that the big picture was a series they were working on that affected her career. The personal side of it ran in a vein much deeper.

"You want to turn here on this road," she instructed as they approached the winding dirt and gravel path that led to the Rices' home.

Living in this region had its benefits, but the feeling of total isolation in the middle of the woods was not one of them. The barren trees formed an entrance way over the road and bordered their route all the way to the house, the branches draping like emaciated arms connected over the path. Abby didn't say anything else to Paul as she stared into the darkness. She then saw the small, antique lanterns that hung only a few inches from the ground, guiding visitors to the front door. The orange glow that emitted from them was faint and served no other purpose than atmosphere.

The two approached the porch in silence. Abby lifted the giant brass fixture that matched the ominous door and tapped it against the heavy oak. A few seconds passed before they heard footsteps. The rapid clicking sound led Abby to believe it was Theresa that approached the foyer. As the door glided open, Mrs. Rice came into view. It looked like she just got home from work. She wore a slim, tailored pantsuit and her makeup looked slightly smudged and wilted. Overall, she was a pretty woman, but her eyes were sallow and small wrinkles graced the area around her mouth. They showed that she wasn't the thirty-something aunt that Abby knew when she was close to Becca. Abby was never quite sure of her age, but she had to be in her late forties.

Paul immediately extended his hand and introduced himself. After brief greetings and introductions with Theresa, Paul went through the same thing again when Jonathan appeared in the door. The couple didn't seem annoyed that Abby and Paul were there, but they didn't seem thrilled. Jonathan invited them into the living room. Abby looked at Paul for a reaction when he walked in. She had been in this home several times years ago, and she was still overcome by the beauty of the home. Paul seemed unaffected by the surroundings. She realized that was the difference between the two of them: Paul was able to separate emotion and work; Abby wasn't as successful.

"We didn't think we would be hearing from you so soon, but I guess you're eager to work on this project?" Jonathan tried to validate why they were here.

"Actually, yes, we are going forward with the story, but there is something else we wanted to discuss," Abby said. She didn't like Jonathan's body language. She could tell by his arms crossed in front of his chest that he was not going to be open to this conversation. Maybe they just came at a bad time.

Jonathan waited for her story without even commenting. He leaned back on the plush pillows that lined the sofa. The dim light cast shadows on his face, making him look older. The twinge of silver in his hair glimmered when he turned his head. Ten years had passed and he was still an attractive man. He wasn't of big stature, but she could tell that he took care of himself and probably still exercised most days. Abby could remember that he was an avid cyclist, but she and Becca were never invited for his rides. He would say that the paths he took were too advanced for the two of them and that they should stay by the lake. Now the man sitting across from her was a man that didn't care about bike rides but only wanted to know why these two people were sitting in his living room.

"Do you want me to explain?" Paul asked.

Abby wanted to jump at the chance to let Paul take over, but on the same note, she wanted to prove to Paul that she was able to handle this. She wasn't Abby Greene sitting here whining about her friend; she was Abby Greene the reporter trying to unravel and understand the new information she had on a particular story.

"No, Paul, that's okay. Let me explain," she said.

The Rices sat there expressionless as Abby started from the beginning. She recounted everything like a broken record from her last visit to this house. Then she said what she didn't want to last time she visited. She told them about Jeremy and how she always wondered if the possibility of murder existed. She kept it brief and waited for one of them to take the next step. Jonathan rose and walked over to the fireplace, resting his arm on the mantle. He turned and faced Abby. Theresa sat motionless with her head down.

"Let me see, Abby. You think that two adults who find a twelve-year-old girl lifeless, a coroner, a funeral director, and a few police officers would all miss some evidence that foul play had been committed? A bottle of pills was found next to her bed, but that doesn't mean anything, all because of your instinct and some teenage kid's murder mystery way of thinking?" he ranted.

Abby wasn't shocked by his response and was ready with an answer. "I'm not saying that is what happened and I am not trying to upset anyone. I just need to know if you ever thought about it and I figured you may be interested in what Jeremy had to say." She hoped her voice didn't sound as quivering as she felt. Her heart pounded in her chest and her face felt like it was on fire.

Jonathan sat back down on the couch and interlaced his fingers, placing them against his forehead. No one said a word as they waited for his reaction.

"You know, Abby, we became very close to Becca for the short time that she lived with us. I wasn't as close to my sister as I would have liked to have been and I didn't get to be as close with her family as I should have. Her illness and death were very hard on me. When we were asked to take Becca in, I found it as an opportunity to make up for lost time. Can you imagine what Theresa and I went through when Becca committed suicide? We had a very hard time dealing with her death, as I am sure you did, too. Sometimes, we blame ourselves and think how we could not have seen the signs or how we could not have been around all of the time to watch her. We want to know why we couldn't prevent such a grisly act from being committed under our roof. We struggled with that for years and still deal with our grief. But we know that something wasn't right in her eyes and it was bad enough that she had to take her life. No one understands suicide or why people do it, and for years, we blamed ourselves. I wish there was something else we could have done, Abby, but we couldn't. Now, just because someone puts an idea in your head, you think you have this new murder case to cover? For as much as we want answers, too, as to why she did it, you can't make up stories to answer your questions or put your mind at ease. And may I ask who you would even have as a suspect? And for what motive?"

Paul then interjected, "We don't have any suspects. That's why we wanted to ask you if—"

Abby cut him off. "No, I do have someone in mind and I wanted to ask you about him."

This statement floored everyone. Paul had no idea that anyone else was involved in this story so he waited just as intently to hear her answer as did Jonathan and Theresa.

"Who, Abby?" Jonathan asked.

"Colin," she said.

Jonathan and Theresa just looked at her, speechless.

"That is just as outrageous as your first brainstorm. Maybe we shouldn't discuss this any further tonight." This was Theresa's first sentence in over twenty minutes. Her tight-lipped grimace did not look welcoming.

Abby and Paul knew they should leave soon

When they finally pulled away from the home, Abby was the first to speak.

"You may want to stop over at my house for a little while. I think I have some explaining to do."

Chapter 9

Abby looked in her refrigerator and found three bottles of Coors Light on the door. She grabbed them and placed them on the table in the living room. The table was a trunk that she picked up at a yard sale. It served a great purpose for storing and serving. If her guests didn't notice the brass hinges, they would never know. Paul didn't seem to care about brass hinges.

"Sorry, I only have three left. We can run out and pick up another six pack if you want to?" she said, motioning to the door.

"No. What I want to know is why I was the only one in that room that didn't know about this Colin character, because it was obvious from the look on their faces that they did. What's going on?"

It's not that he felt left out; it was that he felt misinformed. If Abby had one thing figured out about him by now it's that he wants to be the one in the room who knows about everything that's going on. She thought the Colin angle would just confuse and agitate matters. Now, she thought otherwise.

She went right into the explanation. "When Becca was very young, her parents didn't get along very well with each other. Becca's father, Colin, was a hard worker but a hard drinker as well. Colin's family was involved with selling heavy machinery equipment and the company did quite well. For years, they tried to work Colin into the family business to work towards sharing in the wealth, but he didn't try. To make a long story short, he was too proud to take handouts when he was strapped for money, but he was just as overpowered by alcohol to be unsuccessful on his own. By the time Becca was four years old, he left her and her mother. That is about as much as I know about Colin since Becca didn't have many memories of him. She always wished he would come back, but they never heard from him again."

Paul sat there, nodding during Abby's story. He didn't want to be the one to throw it in her face, but everything he had found out so far was adding up to all of the right conditions in Becca's case. Her father deserted them, her mother passed away, and she was moved into a new environment. There was ample evidence as to why she was depressed. He didn't feel like arguing this point with Abby right now; he knew what the response would be. Instead, he humored her and asked why she thought the father was involved.

"I don't know for sure if he was involved and I never mentioned anything to the Rices, but he was the only immediate family member left in her life. Plus, you saw the reaction I got from them when I brought it up."

Paul didn't want to venture into this territory but he had to. "Yeah, they said that your idea was basically absurd," he said.

Abby perked up in her chair, sitting on the very edge. "You know what, Paul? Theresa was right. It's not good to further discuss this tonight. I am getting tired anyway. It's been a long day," she said, standing up with an exaggerated yawn.

Paul stood up with the remaining beer in his hand. "Come on, Ab. I didn't say *you* were absurd; I was just repeating what Theresa said. Tell me what you think you know about Colin. I'm interested in what you have to say."

"No, I think we should give it a rest. We can look into some things tomorrow if you want. You have to realize, Paul, this was a lot for me today, too. I am sincere when I tell you that I have exhausted all of my talking for the day," she said with half a smile.

He believed her, but knew there was another story that she wanted to tell. However, he realized when it was time to go and knew he would get this story from her at some point anyway. With out any further interrogation, he picked up his coat and headed to the door.

"Listen, don't be upset with me. I promise—"

Her makeshift apology was interrupted by the piercing sound of her phone. She told Paul not to leave.

"Hello?" she answered while glancing at her watch. It was after ten p.m. She wondered who would be calling now. The voice on the other end sounded strained and quiet. "Hello? Who is this? I am having trouble hearing you. Hello?" she reiterated, about to hang up.

"Hi, Abby. I'm sorry to bother you and I know it's late, but it is crucial that I talk to you. I can't get into the details now, but I was wondering when a good time would be for you?" the woman asked.

Abby was very surprised. This was not a call that she expected now or anytime soon.

"I start work early, but maybe we could meet before hand for a quick coffee or something. You know where the Coffee Table is, don't you?" Abby asked.

The entire time, Paul tried every charade to get Abby to clue him in as to who was on the other line. She held up one hand, keeping him on hold and in suspense.

"Great, let's go there early, say eight o'clock? Fine. I will meet you tomorrow. Thanks, Theresa." Abby let out a deep sigh as she replaced the phone in its cradle.

"Theresa? As in Theresa Rice?" Paul asked. His interest was definitely piqued now.

Abby fell back into the living room chair that didn't quite match the rest of the set but looked and felt the most inviting. She shook her head, trying to figure out what just happened and where it was leading.

Without even looking over at Paul, she answered him. "She wants to meet for coffee tomorrow. What ever she wants to tell me is crucial."

Paul's look of bewilderment was the same as Abby's.

Chapter 10

It was just as she figured it would be and just as she preferred. The small coffee shop was empty, except of course for Doreen sweeping behind the counter. There was no staunch competition between her fine brews and Jeb's down the street. They complimented each other quite well. The first was great to sit down and unwind before or after your day; the latter was the usual speed for Abby, since she was always running in and out before work. It also didn't hurt matters that the owner of this little java joint was also Jeb's sister. No matter what spot you stopped in, you were greeted with the same warm and welcoming smile. Today was no exception.

"Good morning, Abby. No work today, I take it?" Doreen asked while filling one of the glass sugar containers. Stopping at The Coffee Table was normally a sign of leisure time.

Abby pulled up one of the wrought iron chairs and placed her bag on it. She peered out the window to look for Theresa. She wiped away some of the condensation on the pane of glass to have a view of the street. The normal morning bustle filled the avenue. Tourists loved stopping in the quaint boutiques that were arranged in a connected row on each side of the two lane road. Abby took the shops for granted but appreciated them when she was looking for a unique gift. The combination of several pots of coffee brewing and the heat of fresh baked goods enveloped the room. There was nothing she could refuse in this place.

"I do have work; I'm just meeting someone here for a quick interview before I go in," she replied. Abby didn't feel like explaining the details and she hoped since she hinted that it was business, Doreen would tend to something else. It wasn't uncommon for Doreen to plop herself down to join in on an approachable conversation.

The manager walked over with a wooden tray. "Well, it's still good to see you this morning. What will it be today? A lemon iced shortbread or blueberry muffin?" the woman asked, her eyes lighting up her rounded face. Her ruddy cheeks were plump but dimpled when she smiled. Her innocent look beckoned Abby to try one of the sugar-laden treats held in front of her.

"I guess the shortbread. Between you and your brother, I'll never lose weight," Abby said and laughed.

"That's because you don't have to. I tell you that all the time. I'll get your latte," Doreen said. She disappeared into the backroom through a pretty floral curtain.

As Doreen pushed the flowered print across the copper rod overhead, the bell above the front door jingled. Theresa walked in, looking business-like as usual. Even though Abby was fully clad for work, she felt underdressed. She greeted Theresa with a smile and rose to meet her before she got to the table.

"Hi, Abby. Oh, no, don't get up," she said, motioning for Abby to stay at the small glass-topped table. "I just love this place. I don't come here often enough. What are you drinking?" she asked. Her eyes were a bit too sparkly this early in the morning.

"Doreen is getting my café latte. Would you like the same?" Abby asked.

Theresa pondered the question and accepted, but asked for non-fat milk.

Abby looked down at her pastry and felt overindulgent. She didn't imagine Theresa would be interested in a fattening muffin or cookie.

Doreen returned with Abby's java brimming with whipped cream.

"Thanks, Doreen. Can we have another one of these with non-fat milk?" she asked.

"And no whipped cream," Theresa added.

Again, Abby sheepishly stirred the heavy whipping cream into her coffee and pushed the cookie around the plate.

Theresa removed her long, black wool coat to reveal the blue and white striped, silk shirt that peeked from beneath when she walked in. The navy pants and perfectly matched shoes looked like something from a designer catalog. Abby's periwinkle sweater and long black skirt didn't seem like as good a choice now as it did this morning. Since dress code wasn't the matter at hand, she figured she should probe Theresa.

"So anyway, I do have to go to work shortly, but you sounded urgent on the phone. Is there something I could help you with?" Abby asked. She hoped Theresa was on her way to work as well and didn't dress like that on a whim.

Doreen exited the room to give them some space and Theresa waited until she did so. There were no other patrons in the café, but she still looked around with suspicion. She then got right to the point.

"I won't keep you long, but I needed to talk to you after yesterday."

Abby pulled her chair closer to the table, nudging the tabletop and spilling some of her latte over the rim.

"This is about yesterday. I want to apologize that I didn't speak up earlier, but as you could tell, Jonathan was visibly upset. You know Becca moved in with us after her mom died. I knew her over the years, being with Jonathan, but we didn't see her and her mom often. This wasn't because we didn't want to, but we both have hectic schedules. Jonathan is always commuting back and forth to Syracuse with his business, and I am constantly on the road with my sales job," she explained. "After Jon's sister's death, we had to take Becca in. She really didn't have any other family. But a short time after Jean's funeral, we received a phone call from

Colin. He didn't even come to his own wife's service, which was a shame in itself, but he was certain to call afterwards to check on Becca," she said.

"Well, that was good, I guess. He should have been there years before and when his wife died, right?" Abby tried to see where this was going.

"That's true, but the sad part was, Colin didn't call to check on how Becca was doing. That's exactly what he said when he called. He just wanted to make sure there was money left for Becca to help support her. Now, of course, he wasn't interested in taking her in himself, but when it came to money, he showed a great deal of interest. For some reason, he thought that Jean left this great inheritance for Becca. I guess that thought sparked enough interest for Colin to come crawling around. When he called, I talked to him. I didn't even let Jonathan know that his brother-in-law tried to get in contact with them, due to the bitter feelings Jonathan had for him. Jonathan was so upset the way it was, dealing with the loss of his sister then trying to help his niece get through her grief. The last thing he would want to hear was someone trying to ask about an inheritance." Theresa paused to sip her coffee. Her fingers laced through the ceramic loop and flashed the huge, glittering gem that Abby never noticed before.

"Was that it? You never told him, and Colin failed to call again?" Abby asked, trying to piece this together.

"He called a few times thereafter, telling me that he was going to attempt to get custody of Becca. I explained that walking out on his family years ago and then coming around once he smelled money was not going to work. He stopped calling. A few months later, Becca committed suicide."

Abby saw where she was going with this but didn't know why this important issue wasn't brought up yesterday when they looked at her like she was crazed when she mentioned murder.

"Did he get in touch with you after the suicide? Did he even come to the wake service?" Abby asked. "I don't remember him there, even though

I never met him. I would have recalled someone pointing out that he was her missing father," Abby said.

Theresa paused then finished her coffee, dabbing her mouth before folding the small napkin and placing it on the saucer's edge. "He called once, wondering if Becca left anything behind so he could have a remembrance. I told him to leave us alone, that he no longer had ties to this family. We never spoke to him again."

Abby wasn't sure what the exact point of this was. She wondered why she would bring this entire story up about Colin if he were eliminated from the picture. Abby came right out and asked. "Theresa, are you saying that you suspect Colin is a murderer?" she whispered, leaning in as close as possible.

"Until you stopped over the other day, I never thought about anything but the unfortunate and saddening fact that Becca ended her own life. We would wrestle with the idea all of the time, wondering why and what we could have done. But something you said the other day just brought back memories of my few run-ins with Colin on the phone. I just want you to know that I am not saying that I think anyone killed Becca, but if there was ever such a suspect, I would look into Colin being a plausible choice. It sounds outlandish, that he would be able to kill his own flesh and blood, but with money involved and his track record of not caring for years, it's not too far out of the ballpark. I guess a reason I never had a deep suspicion before was because the coroner ruled it as a suicide. It was cut and dry, not even a case to investigate. I'm sure they would have noticed foul play, so this murder theory is improbable. But if there is any chance that your friend from the funeral home has a shred of truth to what he said, you know where to look." Theresa sat back in the wiry chair, studying Abby's face for a reaction.

"Wow, I don't know what to say. Do you think I should track Colin down and bring up some questions?" she asked.

"I wouldn't even know where to begin to look for him, to tell you the truth. The last time I talked him, he was living in Pennsylvania, I know that much. Just one thing though, Abby," she pleaded, "don't mention any of this to Jonathan, not even that we talked."

"Okay, but don't you think he would want to know if someone killed his own niece?" This was getting confusing, and Abby was still waiting to see what Theresa had to gain by this meeting of theirs.

"As far as that goes, you really upset him the other day. Like I said, it took a long time to deal with our grief, and to come up with your story and rekindle the old feelings, it wasn't easy for him. I think he wants to leave well enough alone. He dealt with Becca's suicide and is trying to cope with the grim facts the best he can. I don't think he could handle this new twist."

"Will you still be willing to help me out if I need any additional information?" Abby asked. She understood Theresa's point, but if she could get any information from her, it would help. She didn't want to let this be their last meeting and alienate herself.

"Sure, Abby, but right now, I have to get going. I have a call I have to rush to. Thanks for the coffee and please don't talk about this. I just wouldn't be able to live with myself if I didn't divulge this information. If by some slim chance Colin was involved in any way, just be careful. If he could harm his family, who knows what else he is capable of doing. I just wanted to let you in on this information, but I have to get going now. I'll see you, Abby," she said, waving to Doreen as she picked up her coat and left.

Abby just sat there, stunned. The fact that Theresa had Abby pay for her coffee wasn't an issue, but her warning about being careful was the first time Abby thought that she was at any sort of risk. She never thought of it that way. Theresa dominated the conversation and hardly let Abby get a word in edgewise. She spoke her piece and left, basically saying that she doesn't think this was the case, but if anything ever happened, don't say she didn't tell her so. That was a lot to digest. Maybe Theresa felt guilty about never mentioning Colin to anyone, and now that she finally told someone, she felt a weight was lifted. Now it was Abby's weight to bear. Whatever it was, it put Abby on the right track if she wanted to delve into this further.

She finished her coffee and looked out the window, just in time to see Theresa getting into her new Volvo. Doreen tapped Abby on the shoulder and whispered to her as if someone was still there.

"Hmmm, new Volvo and she allows you to pick up the tab?" She smirked, following it with a hearty laugh.

"No, that's fine. She's just an old friend I haven't talked to in a while," Abby said.

After refusing the cherry Danish that Doreen kept pushing on her, she thanked her and headed to work with her mind two steps ahead of herself.

Chapter 11

Abby pulled into the parking lot and raced into the building. She couldn't wait to divulge all of the information that she just received. She had ideas swarming in her head that needed to be sorted out. She knew Paul would understand. On her way into the newsroom, she literally bumped into her news director.

"Oh, hi, Dave, sorry I am a little late," she said, spilling the contents of her bag onto the desk. For as early as she met Theresa at the coffee shop, she still managed to be fifteen minutes late. This usually wasn't a big deal. Today for some reason, Dave thought it was.

"Ab, just try to make it here a little earlier from now on. I need you right now to make some calls to the police station. There is supposed to be some follow-up information on the arson case you reported on the other day. Didn't you hear about that?" he asked, somewhat annoyed.

Abby knew this was coming sooner or later. Even though she wasn't always at the station, her job basically encompassed her every waking hour. If she wasn't working and saw something news-worthy happening, she always called into the station. Much of her free time was spent reading newspapers and magazines. She kept up with the current news and was aware of updates before most people. This wasn't the case during the past few days. She wished that she could spend the majority of her time researching her current project. As far as she was concerned, the project wasn't the suicide series; it was Becca. The series was important, and they would get it done, but the tie-in was much greater.

She agreed with Dave and picked up her phone as soon as she sat down. He smiled in approval and went back to his office. He couldn't stay aggravated at her for long.

She hadn't gotten far with the police department when Paul walked over.

"Dave's a little cranky today, don't you think?" he asked.

"Why? Did he say something about me being late? I didn't think it was that big of a deal. I am usually here early, as a matter of fact, but he won't take that into consideration. And what about weekends?" she defended herself.

"Relax, relax," Paul said. "I was just mentioning that he was not in the greatest mood. You are not the only one he had a short fuse with today. Enough about that, how did you're breakfast meeting go?"

"Surprisingly well." She gave Paul all of the details and could read the expression on his face that he was as intrigued and shocked as she was.

"Wow. I will have to talk to Jeremy about this later. He never mentioned much about Colin, but I can check to see if he remembers anything about him and if he showed up around the funeral home. Are you on until after the six today?" he asked.

"No, I'm only scheduled for a few hours. I guess that is why Dave is a bit ticked since he needs a lot done by noon. I want to try to head up to Gore for a few hours before it gets dark. I didn't do much skiing this year and I would like to get some in before the winter is over."

"Nice, have fun. Be careful, though," he warned.

"What do you mean *be careful?*"

"I mean that if you are skiing by yourself, just be careful. You know it is always better to ski with at least one person. It's a nice day today, though. Enjoy yourself."

The remainder of the morning flew by. At twelve-thirty p.m., Abby ran home to gather her skis and equipment. The beautiful day seemed to take a turn. The sky looked white and billowy with the sign of looming snow clouds. The snowfall was usually welcomed, but Abby preferred an already packed snow mountain and lots of sunshine.

Before heading to Gore, she planned on making a stop on Hartford Drive for a few minutes. The road winded and curved until it reached the top of the hill. There sat a quaint farmhouse with the weathered but inviting front porch. The swing undulated in the wind, making the familiar tapping against the bleached aluminum siding. She knocked twice on the door before walking in. He was usually there. Sure enough as she walked in, Michael Greene was standing at the stove with an oversized oven mitt, clutching an iron skillet on the stove.

"Abby girl, just in time. How about a fried cheese sandwich?" he asked, pointing to the sizzling white mass in front of him.

"Dad, that's good: a fried cheese sandwich. I thought you said you were going to start eating healthier. I know I am trying to." She didn't want to admit how good the greasy food sputtering in the pan smelled.

"It's feel-good food and it's cold out," he tried to justify. "How about just half?"

"Okay," Abby relented.

She didn't visit her dad as often as she should. He refused to move out of this house after her mother died. It was hard for both of them, but even tougher for him. When her mom passed away after her second heart attack, Abby was away at school. The counselor helped Abby deal with her grief, but she still missed her everyday. Her dad, on the other hand, chose not to talk to anyone. His grief was even harder to manage, but he was doing better now. He cooked for himself, even though it may be a cheese or steak sandwich. He tried. The one thing Abby didn't like was that he didn't take care of himself the way he should. Both he and Abby made a pact that they would try to improve their eating habits and exercise. Abby wasn't going to point a finger too quickly, though. Lately, she wasn't holding up her end of the bargain.

"So anyway, how is the story going at work?" her father asked as he slid the golden sandwich onto a blue-rimmed plate. Abby hadn't revealed too much of what was going on. He knew that she was busy at work with her new assignment. His first concern was if she could handle it, considering the topic.

She did not get into the details about what she found out about Becca's death or the circumstances surrounding it. She knew he would worry about her and how she was handling everything. "The series is coming together. It's going to be a semi-permanent feature every two weeks. Paul and I are developing the suicide topic, but we will eventually move on to other teen matters." As far as she was concerned, investigating Becca's death was the only subject she wanted to work on.

"Paul, Paul, Paul. Boy, I always hear his name mentioned in all of your stories. It sounds like maybe you have something more with him than reporting?" her dad joked.

Abby smiled and shook her head. During the recent days since they started working closer together, she had really gotten to know Paul. She didn't think that she talked about him all of the time, but it was obvious that she brought up his name more times than not in her conversations. It was normal to do that, she thought. He was involved in this now as deep as she was. Whether she would admit to herself or not, she looked forward to seeing Paul everyday, but she was not going to admit this to her father.

"Dad, we are just friends. I work on this with him everyday, so of course I am going to mention him from time to time. He is a good guy and he knows a lot about the industry. I learn from him, too," she said, trying to state her case.

Her dad raised his eyebrows and shrugged. "I would still like to meet this Paul if he is such a good guy. Invite him over one of these times," he offered.

Her father walked over to his front window and pushed the yellowed lace curtains aside. Many things here were just as her mother had left them. She knew why there were still many feminine touches around the house: her dad wanted to keep Abby's mom's presence in some form in the house; he couldn't bear to get rid of reminders of her. Abby looked at him standing by the window. After years of construction work, his face seemed to have a year-round redness. His crew cut hairstyle never altered from all of the years that Abby could remember. In her eyes, he didn't change much. The only thing that did change was the sadness reflected in his eyes. It hadn't been many years since his wife died, but some days he would think it was just yesterday. Abby felt the same way, too. She tried to be strong for him. One fact that Abby resented was that people she loved were taken from her too soon. That might explain why she was hesitant to get close to anyone. If she wasn't close to people, she couldn't miss them as much if they were gone. Her dad, of course, was an exception, and now Paul was falling into that category, too.

Her dad stooped down to get a better perspective of the sky. "Did you say you were going skiing today?" he said without breaking his gaze into the snow-laden clouds. He didn't give Abby a chance to respond and marched forward with more fatherly advice. "You better be careful; it looks like a pretty heavy storm is coming through. Maybe you should go another day."

Abby laughed to herself. That was her second warning of the day. "No. It's not often I have half a day. I will be okay. I am only going up for a few hours. It's not supposed to start snowing until tonight, I believe. I will head back if it starts to snow hard."

She placed her dish in the sink and kissed her dad on the cheek. After all of these years, his Old Spice aftershave was another thing he never changed. Abby liked that. A strong hug from her dad and the spicy smell made her feel safe and secure no matter what.

"I'll call you later," she said and headed to her car.

Her dad leaned against the doorframe and watched her until she disappeared over the hill. Her Honda coasted down the steep incline, and regardless of the ominous sky, she felt good about the day.

Chapter 12

For living so close to a ski resort, Abby didn't get to hit the slopes nearly as much as she wished. When she was younger, she would always have a season pass, but she also didn't have a real job and other responsibilities at the time. Most of her friends that she would ski with moved away, and she didn't mind going by herself, but it was nice to have a buddy to enjoy the slopes with. She would have to ask Paul to go one of these times.

Within in twenty minutes, she reached the road that led to the mountain. She figured that with the impending snowfall and that it was midweek, the slopes wouldn't be that crowded. Even when it was crowded, it never seemed excessively brimming with people since Gore Mountain boasted more than sixty trails. The breathtaking scenery of this mountain and this region couldn't be beat. Abby considered herself lucky to have it in her backyard.

By the time she finally made it to the Northwoods Gondola, three people alerted her of the approaching storm. Abby was looking forward to relaxing during her solo ride up the mountain. The few minutes it took to get to the top made Abby feel like she was flying through a winter wonderland. The ride allowed her to relax until someone opened the door and handed her the skis and poles from the back of the vessel. When Abby was at the bottom of the slope, another man was standing near the lift. Abby was glad he didn't ride up with her; it wasn't often she got to enjoy the gondola by herself. Maybe he wanted to do the same thing, since he just got off the next car that came to the top. He was looking at the trail map near the ski patrol station. Abby hoped he wasn't following her same route. She was selfish and wanted all of this to herself today.

The summit elevation was thirty-six-hundred feet. Due to this fact, the snow had already started up there.

Abby tossed her skis to the ground and snapped in. She trudged over to the fork where she could choose her trail and made her way over to one of her favorites, Wood Lot. It was intermediate, but it was long.

As she pushed off, her skis turned with ease in the powder. The wind in her ears and the gentle swoosh of her skis made a pleasant sound. The snow was coming down a little harder, forming a pristine white blanket in front of her that obstructed her vision. Abby hoped it would lessen as she made her way down the winding trail. She stopped to pull her goggles down. When she did, she noticed the same man with the black pants and jacket with a slim green stripe on his sleeve, weaving his way down the trail. Abby figured she was lucky to be skiing with so few people the way it was, and that she shouldn't be greedy.

Saddle Lodge was a half way point, and she glided over to one of the log benches to take a rest. Seconds later, Green Stripe, as she labeled him, was taking a break as well.

The snow was starting to pick up to the point where visibility was getting difficult. The precipitation wasn't as billowy now. It seemed to be mixed with a pelting, freezing rain. Between not being able to see and icy conditions, Abby decided that if it didn't let up by the time she reached the bottom, she would have to make her first run her only run.

Rested, she headed over to Otter Slide until she approached the top of one of the black diamond slopes. Although a seasoned skier, Abby was more confident on the intermediate slopes. Besides the fact the she could barely see, it unnerved her that green stripe was not too far behind. There were many choices available coming down the mountain, and it was odd that this man was in Abby's exact path. This guy was probably nothing to worry about, but his parallel paths seemed too coincidental. Plus, he didn't try to pass her. She knew that if she took Wild Air, it would allow her to get to the bottom faster and she now wanted to get to the bottom as soon as possible for several reasons.

She sharply turned her skis and headed down one of the most trying slopes the mountain had to offer. She took her time and battled with the steep, vertical drop. She concentrated and watched her turns. The slope was beginning to develop a thin crust of ice that caused her to dig in harder. She heard a swooshing approach behind her, and moved to the side of the hill to let the skier pass. Before she could even turn and head to one side, the skier came so close to her that his skis skimmed her edge and knocked Abby off balance. She fell to the ground, but due to the fact that she wasn't skiing at a high rate of speed, she only slid about ten or fifteen feet and was able to dig her poles into the packed snow to stop. Her pole fell in front of her and was the first thing she hit before she hit the snow. The warm blood that flowed from her lip dripped onto the snow, marring the perfect surface. As she lifted her head to look in front of her, she saw the green stripe stopped about twenty feet in front of her. He was waiting for her to cascade down the hill and must have been surprised when she stopped.

A girl stopped behind her to see if she was okay. She helped her up and Abby brushed the snow off her dark gray ski pants and turned to see that green stripe was gone. She made her way back down the mountain, going side to side as slow as possible. She didn't want to take any chances. With every curve of the path, she expected to see green stripe waiting. She tried to convince herself that he was just another skier that happened to take all of the same paths as Abby and just happened to ski out of control when he passed her. Somehow, she didn't do a good job of convincing herself. She wanted to make it down the mountain safely. The snow was so heavy now that if he were two feet in front of her, she wouldn't see him. Everyone warned her about skiing today, but the weather seemed to be the least of her concerns.

Abby made it to the lodge and stopped in front of her locker. She popped out of her skis and fumbled with the combination. Her teeth clenched her puffy mittens and her hands shook. The tip immediately became soaked with blood as she forgot about her busted lip. She knew the shaking wasn't from the cold; it was going to take a lot to rid her of this rattled feeling. The slim cord gave way and she shoved her skis into the holder to secure them. After bringing a cold hand to her cheek, she determined that her face wasn't bleeding, but the skin underneath her fingers was tender to the touch. She would definitely have an unattractive bruise or scrape to match her swollen lip.

"That's a nasty scrape on your face. Your lip looks pretty busted up, too," someone from ski patrol said as he approached. "What happened?"

Abby did not especially want to get into the details. She knew she would be telling the story over and over. "It's nothing." She undid the band in her hair and let some strands fall over the side of her face to cover it. "With the storm and everything, I guess someone just didn't see me. It's no big deal," she said and turned to gather her things in the lodge.

"It's a good thing you're leaving now. The weather is going to get worse instead of better. Have a safe drive home and take care of that face," he said.

She loosened her boots and stomped into the lodge. The bathroom mirror reflection didn't portray such a bad picture. Her face was more reddish than scraped.

After grabbing her things, she fought against the storm with her skis just to get to her car. She imagined what the ride home was going to be like.

* * * *

Abby sighed with relief when she arrived in front of her apartment. The usual twenty-minute ride took her well over an hour. She tossed everything, including her skis onto the couch. She plopped down in the chair next to her answering machine. Her heavy, insulated jacket was making her sweat now, and she shrugged out of it while she waited for the playback of the six messages waiting for her. She knew that most would be from her father and maybe Paul, both concerned about her commute home. The biggest surprise was when only two had her dad's voice and one from Paul. The other three were not welcomed messages.

With the same shaking hand, she picked up the phone and then glanced at the door to make sure it was locked.

Chapter 13

For several days, Jeremy pondered what he revealed to Paul. The coincidence of Abby's involvement in the situation was a sign that he had to let it resurface again. It was years ago, but the vivid details haunted Jeremy for the past few days.

When Becca was prepared for her viewing, it was the first time Jeremy was exposed to seeing someone so close to his age touched by the hand of death. Bob Franklin was Jeremy's mentor, and Jeremy knew he was only trying to protect him by not wanting him around during the preparation. Jeremy wished that Bob was more insistent. The scenario disturbed him greatly. He also knew that he would have to deal with situations like this if he was going to be in the business. The marks he had found puzzled him. The explanation he received was plausible, but his satisfaction in accepting that information wavered. He was sure that Bob Franklin wondered, too. However, he never discussed it with him after that day. It was years ago that this happened. Back then, just starting out in the business, Jeremy didn't want to press his luck. He was happy to be given a chance that may propel his career.

As Jeremy walked to the back house of the funeral home, he decided they were both mature adults now. Reintroducing this topic would not be absurd. It would also prepare Bob if Paul and Abby started asking questions.

The back house wasn't attached to the funeral home; it was located directly behind it. A waiting cadaver was in a hearse outside it. Jeremy opened the door of the black station wagon and slid the body bag onto the gurney. The thick, gray plastic made a zipping sound as it slid from the upholstered interior of the car onto the unfolded, metal carrier. The idea that the greatest symbol of death loomed beneath his hands did not bother him. Jeremy was able to separate his work from his feelings. The bloated corpse enclosed in its temporary plastic resting place needed to be embalmed and prepared. That was his job. He also knew that the man left behind a wife and two children. He knew if he let his mind wander further than that, his emotions would take over.

The wheels turned with a squeak as he leaned his body weight against the metal bar, pushing towards the door and fumbling with his key. He should have had the door unlocked already. It was best not to be seen outside, transporting the body. People knew it happened, but no one likes to see it. The main house does a good job of masking the view from the road. The odds were that no one was going to see him even if they were passing by. He steadied the cart with one hand and fished in his pocket with the other. The overloaded key ring jangled in his hand as he searched for the right one. The air was cold tonight, and the few short minutes he was outside caused him to gasp from his icy breath reaching his lungs.

The mortuary inside was cold, but it felt quite tropical compared to being outside this winter Monday. Jeremy shed his jacket and flipped on the lights and the radio. Bob was out of town today, so Jeremy was on his own. He didn't mind.

Jeremy put on his apron, gloves, and mask after preparing the instruments. He unzipped the bag to reveal a pallid corpse.

As he leaned forward to arrange the man's arm on the table, he felt a cold draft dancing against his neck. Under his apron, Jeremy's collared shirt was covered by a maroon sweater. This would usually make him warm by now. He turned to see what caused the icy feeling on his skin. The room itself was very plain and sterile as this was where body fluids were drained and lacerations patched up.

Near the door where he entered was a window. He walked over and moved the room darkening shades to discover the pane had been broken.

A tree branch was jutting through, slightly scraping the blinds. He tried to look out the window to see if the tree had fallen, but it was too dark to notice. He would have to tell Bob when he returned. The branch continued to grate against vinyl, making Jeremy uneasy. It was very rare that he was bothered or spooked by what he did and the elements surrounding him. The roaring wind outside, the cold, night air that poured into the violated window, and a lifeless body setting in front of him made him uneasy tonight. It may have been that he had so much on his mind the past few days that put him on edge this evening.

"This is crazy, Jer," he said aloud to himself. He turned up the radio and switched away from the mellow station that he usually kept tuned.

As he approached the table, the scraping turned into a rustling. He swung around, knocking the instruments off of the porcelain table. He could have sworn he heard someone walking. The wooded area behind the structure was home to many animals, and it could have been something that scampered by. Regardless of what it was, he couldn't do this tonight. Everything was a little too taxing on his mind lately, and it was starting to get to him. He would have to prepare everything again anyway.

He covered the body and slid it into refrigeration. He would come back down at the crack of dawn when his mind was rested and the shadows weren't playing tricks on him. He cleaned up as fast as possible and inventoried the room one last time before he turned out the lights and closed the door.

The status of the roads didn't change from when he arrived. It was snowing all day, but there was a lull now. He thought the road crews would be out plowing when they could, but they, like everyone else, probably figured that the worst was yet to come. Jeremy felt confident in his SUV, something needed to navigate during winters in Watertown.

He cranked the music and headed up Sutton Hill. He placed his palm against the vent near the steering wheel. The warm heat emanating from the plastic slots felt good against his chilled skin, but it would take sometime until the entire Explorer heated. Even though he trusted his vehicle in adverse conditions, he would always take it slow. If he hit ice, it didn't matter what he was driving. He hated when people would drive like they were invincible, just like the person approaching behind him. The lights on the pickup ascending the hill bounced in his rearview mirror as it plowed up the steep incline.

"Asshole," Jeremy said out loud. "Well, you can wait, buddy, because today is not my day."

Between watching the road and his mirror, he noticed the truck wasn't slowing down.

"What the hell?" he yelled as the early model pickup bumped him from behind. If they were descending the hill, he could understand that someone lost control, but he had no idea what this person was doing. He clutched the wheel and tried to make out the identity of the driver. The blinding fog lights revealed a shadow behind the wheel.

He crested the hill and headed for the hairpin turn, knowing that on the other side of the trees was a drop off that prevented people from driving recklessly during normal weather. With snow-covered roads, it was foolish to even try to drive this route. Jeremy slowed and pumped the breaks as he slid around the corner. The truck hit him again and caused the Explorer to spin out of control. Jeremy pulled on the steering wheel and tried to steady himself back onto the road, but the icy conditions prevented his attempt. He pushed against the steering column as he hoped the trees would slow his vehicle.

Chapter 14

"Let me see this face of yours." Paul grimaced as he studied Abby's cheek. He exaggerated a fall against the desk and held his chest. "That's awful. I think you should rush to the doctor," he said with great drama.

"Very funny," she said, swatting Paul's shoulder. "It looked worse yesterday. I think I covered it well today."

The entire situation that happened on the slopes the day before sounded more dramatic last night when she recounted the details to Paul. It wasn't that he didn't believe she was run off the hill, just not on purpose. This aggravated her that he discounted any possibility that someone would try to intentionally harm her. He was right about the inclement conditions playing a huge role, but he also wasn't there and didn't sense what she did. As for the phone calls, he said it could have been him not hanging up in time when he realized she wasn't home. She didn't feel like arguing her point since he had an answer for each odd situation that she described.

Abby turned her cheek as she glanced in her compact mirror. Her face didn't look as harsh as she had described. She guessed that she should be thankful for that and tried to change the subject.

"Hey, have you talked to Jeremy about that whole Colin deal?" she asked.

"No, actually, I haven't had a chance. I did call him yesterday and left a message, but he never called me back. I will try him again tonight," he said with little enthusiasm.

Abby knew that Paul was skeptical about the information concerning Colin. She was going to wait to hear what Jeremy had to say about that before she brought it up again.

Dave walked over and interrupted them. "Paul, there was a message for you on the news line answering service. It was from a Mr. Gerald Greish. It sounded urgent, if you want to give him a call back," he said before returning to his office.

Abby recognized the name immediately and knew that Paul did not receive regular calls from Jeremy's dad.

The concern she had was mirrored on Paul's face. He acted calm as usual. "I wonder what that is all about. I guess I should give him a call," he said, walking over to his desk.

Abby went about her morning tasks but kept an eye on Paul from the assignment desk. She watched as he slowly went from a standing position to being slumped in his chair with one hand clutching the receiver, the other grasping his head. She didn't hear a word of the conversation, but could tell from Paul's awkward body language that something was wrong. He didn't exude his usual confidence and control; he was visibly shaken. Abby approached his desk with caution, watching as he tapped his interlaced hands against his forehead.

"Paul, what is it?" she asked, with a gentle and calming tone. She was shocked to see his eyes filling with tears once he looked at her. His empty glare on the computer screen and silence made Abby even more anxious. She grabbed the back of his chair and leaned in closer. She could hear his increased respiration but he said nothing. "Paul, are you okay?"

He paused for several seconds before revealing what he found out. "That was Jeremy's dad. Jer never came home last night," he said. "This morning, Mr. Greish called me to see if I have heard from him. It turns out someone else got back to him first. The police just called Mr. Greish. They found Jeremy's Explorer off of Sutton Hill Road." He paused for a moment and shook his head in disbelief. This time, it was a greater challenge to hold back the tears.

The face that Abby usually saw filled with certainty looked so vulnerable now. She could figure out the rest of the news but waited for Paul to continue.

"He is dead, Abby. He was dead when they found him this morning. They think that he died instantly from massive head trauma. I can't believe this is happening. But, I…uh…I have to go home. Let me go talk to Dave—"

Abby interrupted him. "Go, Paul. Go see his parents. I'll talk to Dave and explain the situation. I am so sorry. I don't know what to say. Call me when you have a chance or if you need anything."

"Thanks, Ab," he murmured and walked out the door.

Abby stood there in amazement. She knew for a fact that Paul was not on the same wavelength as she was and could not possibly have the same thoughts running through his head, but she knew what he was going through. She knew how he felt after just finding out about the death of his close friend. It was ironic that he had to experience the same thing she did. But that was not what amazed Abby. Ever since the story about Becca resurfaced, it seemed anyone armed with related information was at risk. Abby knew the skiing accident was no accident. She doubted Jeremy's car wreck happened due to bad weather. There was another bad element here and Abby felt fear.

She ran outside to try to catch Paul before he left. Strangely, the day outside was beautiful. He was just about to get into his car when he turned to see Abby running out the door. The sun bounced off Paul's tear-streaked face when he faced her.

"Be careful, Paul," she cautioned. She planned on saying more, but knew it wasn't the right time.

He looked down for a second and nodded. "I will. Thanks. I'll call you later," he said and got into his car.

Abby ran back into the station to talk to Dave. She worried about what could possibly happen next, but knew in her mind that there was no getting out of this now. Someone didn't like that the story of Becca was being told, and Abby had to find out why. The past two days had convinced her of many things, even though they were not all things that she wanted to know. Now, she didn't have many choices.

Abby explained the situation to Dave. Of course, he was already aware of it. He had enough sense not to send Abby to cover the story. For as much as she would usually plead to assist on a story for experience, the last thing she would want to do was cover this. Dave didn't know the extent of her ties to Jeremy, but he knew they were acquainted.

Abby wanted to finish work and go home. She wanted to go home and wait for Paul to call to make sure that everything was okay. She had a bad feeling.

Abby made it through the rest of her day and prepared to go home while Dave stayed at the station.

"Take care, Abby. Tell Paul we won't expect to see him for a few days. We will manage," he said. For someone who was usually high strung and always worried about the next story, he was being very compassionate.

Abby headed home.

When she walked in the door, she grabbed an iced tea and propped herself up on the couch where she didn't plan on moving for the rest of the night. She knew she should call her dad and give him an update on what happened over the past two days, but she just couldn't bring herself to do it yet.

Abby surfed through the channels without even paying attention to what was on; there were more thoughts channeling through her mind. The drama she experienced the day before seemed trivial now. Abby was convinced that someone tried to hurt her. The thought crossed her mind how everything meshed together over the past few weeks and how similar it all was.

She sat, playing along with Jeopardy and checking the clock every few minutes. She decided to try Paul's apartment. He may have gotten home but didn't want to talk. However, Abby knew he needed to talk to someone. After several rings, his calming voice on the answering machine picked up. Abby didn't want to seem like she was pestering him, so she decided not to leave a message.

After being home for quite sometime, she finally decided to get changed. She slid into her nylon pants and favorite sweatshirt. With her hair pulled away from her face and favorite slippers on her feet, she immediately felt at ease. An oversized mug filled with tomato soup and crackers gave her some solace. She had phone calls to make and questions to think of, but right now her focus was the soothing, warm creaminess of the soup as she brought the ceramic cup to her lips. Her feet were curled under her and the only light in her living room was the glare from the television as well as the small lamp next to the phone. It was shining on the receiver, beckoning it to ring.

After an endless search of the channels, Abby was happy to find she only missed twenty minutes of one of her favorite movies of all times. *The Great Gatsby* was on The Movie Channel, and she could never get enough of this movie. There was an awful remake done a few years ago that didn't even come close to the grand performance of Redford in her favorite classic.

She ran her fingers over her cheek. The swelling was almost gone now.

* * * *

The clanking sound was the spoon from her mug as she kicked the trunk in front of her. Redford was lying face down in his pool and Abby's answering machine was just picking up. She must have dozed off.

"Hi, Ab, it's me. I just wanted to see if you…" Paul started, trailing off.

Abby didn't give the machine a chance to record any more of his message. She cleared her throat a few times and pressed the receiver against her face. "Hey, how are you? Are you all right?"

"I guess so. I'm so wiped out. I don't mean to bother you so late."

Abby turned to look at the clock. She must have dozed off longer than she thought. It was after eleven already.

"I was going to stop over, but I figured I should just wait until tomorrow," he continued.

"No, no, why don't you come over now, just to sit and talk for awhile," she said, trying to sound welcoming and not still in her sleeping stupor.

She got off of the couch and tried to shake a cramp that settled in her leg. Abby looked in the oval mirror above the small pedestal table near the door and grimaced at what she saw. Her eyes were smudged with gray eye shadow and her wayward hair was sticking out of her loose ponytail.

"I'm actually in front of your house on my cell phone. I planned on coming right over, but when I realized how late it was, I figured I should call first so I wouldn't disturb you…and to make sure you didn't mind," Paul said with a bit of doubt in his voice.

"I am unlocking the door now. Just come in," she said.

Abby gave up on her appearance. There wasn't much she could do now. She was able to pull the loose strands together and secure them tightly and wipe a tissue underneath her eyes. Just as she did this, she heard a slight tap at the door then watched as the doorknob turned. She walked over just as Paul entered.

"Hey," was all she could say. She was planning on using all these meaningful words of comfort, but "hey" and a hug seemed appropriate now. He squeezed her tight and burrowed his head into her neck. Abby didn't expect this from him and she had her hands in an awkward position.

She grabbed his back and shoulders and reciprocated the embrace. His grip squeezed all breath out of her, not to mention sending shivers through the rest of her body. Once they broke away, he was dabbing at his eyes.

"I'm sorry," he said. "I needed that. Please, if I am bothering you, seriously, I can just talk to you tomorrow," he said, going right back into apologizing.

"Paul, stop it. Just don't mind the way I look. As you can tell, I'm in my comfy clothes," she said, throwing her arms up in despair.

"You look fine," he said, shrugging out of his coat.

Abby looked at his face. She could tell he must have been crying most of the evening. No matter what happened, it would take a lot for him to look bad. He took a seat on the chair and hung his head. She waited for him to do the explaining.

"Abby, it was just awful. I mean, I know you know what it's like to lose a friend, but it is just so hard," he repeated. "I was at the Greishs' for most of the day. God, are they a mess. His mother is the one that got the call to come over to the hospital. They wouldn't tell her anything on the phone. Jer's dad got on the phone and tried to find out what was going on. He said even though they wouldn't reveal anything, he knew something was wrong."

"So he died at the hospital?" Abby asked.

"No, he died at the scene. He was dead when they found him. The ambulance took him there anyway. It must have been pretty bad. I saw his car and it was twisted. A tree went through his windshield and pinned him into the seat. It was violent. They are not even going to have an open casket."

Abby was impressed that Paul could recount these details to her without breaking down. She was sure it was still the shock and exhaustion that were taking over now. She tried to keep him talking.

"What happened exactly? Did he hit a tree?"

"They are going to try to reconstruct the scene, but they think the icy roads were to blame. There were no witnesses, as far as they know, but he drove right off of the embankment. You would think the trees would stop his car from plowing off of the drop-off, but that factor was the very thing that killed him. There was a tree knocked down from the last storm." Paul sighed and shook his head, not picking it up to look at Abby.

"You don't have to say anything else. I'm so sorry." Abby paused and tried to shift the conversation. "When is the viewing?"

"Huh. That's the funny thing, isn't it? Who prepares the one who usually prepares?"

"You don't mean they are having his service at Franklin where he worked?"

"No, Bob Franklin is taking it pretty hard, too. He was shocked when he heard the news. He knew Jeremy for a long time. Bob treated him like he was his son. It's bad for everyone. I was going to stay there later, but several family members were in and out all day and I'm sure they are going to try to get some sleep sooner or later, so I thought I would leave. That was the hardest. While I was at the house, I was busy trying to console everyone and answer the phone that wouldn't stop ringing. Once I got into my car, it gave me time to think. I should have called him, or maybe we could have been out somewhere that wouldn't lead him to drive on that road."

Abby knew all too well that these were normal reactions. She was sure Jeremy's family was probably doing the same thing. She walked over and sat on the arm rest of the chair and rubbed Paul's shoulder. "You can't blame yourself. No one can put the blame on themselves. It's a tragedy what happened, but it's not your fault. I'm sure Jeremy wouldn't want you faulting yourself for it. Hold on, let me get you some tissues." It pained Abby to see Paul sobbing. It was grueling to watch someone that she cared about hurt so much, and even more difficult that it revisited many memories for her.

She stared longingly into her kitchen cabinet, thinking of Paul's pain. She received a bottle of wine as a Christmas gift one year that was more expensive than what she was used to drinking. She found the bottle and dusted it off with her sleeve. She was saving it for a special occasion, but when did something ever come up that was deserving of that? The least she could do was share it with Paul.

"Did you eat? Do you want something? I really don't cook, but I am excellent when it comes to ordering pizza," she said, trying to get him to smile.

He leaned back on the couch. "I'm not hungry. This will work for now," he said, acknowledging the slender bottle she placed on the table.

Abby thought she did a good job of getting Paul's mind off of the subject at hand. He seemed to have calmed down from the time he walked into her apartment. After several glasses of wine, Abby felt more at ease sitting there. She forgot about her baggy sweatshirt and how unkempt her appearance may have looked. It was starting to get late, but she didn't want Paul to leave. They talked about Jeremy and Becca. Not just their untimely deaths, but about the friendships they had with each of them.

Abby loved Paul's enthusiasm for life. His perfect smile would then evolve into a smirk, turning up the corner of one side of his mouth. He listened to Abby when she talked, sympathized, and laughed with her. This friendship was one good thing that was developing out of this experience. She played with the idea of leaving the conversation where it was, but against better judgment, she went ahead with her next question.

"So, Paul, let me ask you something." She tried to be light-hearted about the matter to introduce it into their conversation that was flowing so well. "Between my skiing incident the other day and Jeremy's accident, don't you think it all falls too close to everything that we found out?" She cringed in expectance of his response.

The serene expression on his face changed and was replaced with the same reddened, tense look he arrived with. "Abby, wait a minute. Someone ran into you by accident during near-blizzard conditions while skiing. Icy weather and poor visibility probably played the same role with Jeremy. You might want to cool it with your conspiracy theories," he admonished. He tilted his glass and drank every last drop of the deep burgundy vintage. "When you don't like the outcome of situations, you can't make up your own stories so you can have answers for them. Bad things happen to people everyday. If someone dies, it doesn't always revolve around a murder plot," he finished.

Abby didn't respond. His words were like a stinging hand against her face. She didn't mean to upset him, but she wanted him to at least see the same connections she was making. The one-track mind that she developed now was something she couldn't change. Maybe everything looked suspicious, but to her, it was better to prove it wrong than have it be right.

He was waiting for her rebuttal, but she realized that the clock reflecting one a.m. and the alcohol they both consumed over the past few hours wouldn't make for a friendly argument. She also took into consideration that Paul was grieving. She could help him by letting him do that and for now, not arguing with him.

"I'm sorry," she said. She didn't say she was wrong, she just changed the subject. He seemed to go with it.

Paul yawned several times and Abby figured it was time to put everything to rest for the night. She hoped he would go along with her next suggestion.

"You know what, it's late. Why don't you just stay here tonight? It's probably not a good idea to drive home. I'll wake you up early if you want. I'm still going into work tomorrow. You're not, right?"

"I don't know. It might help me get my mind off of things."

Abby hoped he wouldn't say that. She knew that the station covered the accident, and Paul would see that. He didn't need a reminder to make things worse than they already were. The viewing the following day would be hard enough.

She went into her closet to pull out an extra blanket and pillow. She placed it on the couch and insisted that he get some rest. Without refusal, he kicked off his shoes and plopped back onto the sofa, pulling the blanket over him and fluffing the pillow. Abby stood there for a second, staring at him. He was curled up and facing the couch, sulking away from her. Whether he knew she was right or not, he needed sleep. She thought it best for him to be left alone for now. She needed sleep, too.

Figuring he was out as soon as he hit the pillow, she turned off the lights and whispered "good night."

* * * *

Abby awoke to the sound of trickling and a strong aroma. She heard shuffling then the television being turned on. She glanced at her clock and saw that it was only six-thirty in the morning. She felt as if she just hit the pillow. Paul must have found her coffee maker that she rarely used, but a strong cup of coffee didn't sound like a bad idea right now.

If she thought that she looked unappealing last night, what would Paul think this morning with her tired eyes and smudged make-up from the night before? Her attempts were futile, so the most she could manage was to brush her teeth and splash some cold water on her face. It *was* first thing in the morning, after all.

Paul had on his jeans from the night before but had shed the button-down shirt that he went to sleep in. The cuffs on his pant legs reached down to his heels, and his white t-shirt revealed strong, well-defined arms that weren't too bulky. He looked good.

"Good morning. I hope you don't mind that I rooted around, looking for your coffee maker. And I also found these fresh pastries from the bakery," he said.

Abby laughed as he slid a Pop-tart in front of her. The filling burned her tongue as she nibbled at it.

"Thanks for everything last night. Good choice to make me stay, I needed that," he said, motioning to the couch. He slurped from the steaming cup and then placed it on the counter. "After this, I have to get going. I know you are going to say no, but I am going into work for a little while today. I think it will keep my mind off of things. I plan on going over to Jer's parents' home after, and I want to stop over at Franklin's. He was very close to him, and I want to see how he is doing, too."

So that was it. Abby saw Paul's vulnerable side last night, but now he was back to worrying about everyone else. But that was Paul.

She told him she would see him at work later. She knew the next few days would be up and down, and she prepared herself for it. Then, Paul would have to listen to her whether he liked it or not.

She couldn't help but stare at his arm as he reached across the counter to grab a dishcloth. He wiped up the coffee ring under his cup and placed both in the sink.

He ran his fingers through his tousled hair. "Boy, I must look wonderful this morning

Abby just laughed.

Chapter 15

"Oh, I appreciate you asking, and yes, you're right, I wouldn't be able to do it. If there is else anything I can assist with for you and your family, please let me know.... I'm so sorry, Mrs. Greish. This pains me greatly, too. He is really going to be missed... Okay, then, I will talk to you later, take care."

Bob Franklin placed the phone back into the holder. He sat at his desk, drumming his pencil against the edge. He hoped that he sounded compassionate. Being in this business, it was easy to talk about death because it's what he saw everyday. But this time it was Jeremy. He got an empty feeling in his stomach when he thought about it. He didn't expect the family to want to have the viewing at the funeral home. Frankly, he wasn't sure he could handle it. It was considerate of them to tell him they would be holding it at Risher Funeral Home. The entire situation made him feel uneasy.

When the phone rang, it startled him, as well as finding out who was the person on the other end of the line.

"Oh, hi, how are you?" he greeted, a bit surprised. He knew of Abby Greene through Jeremy and his friend Paul, but he wasn't expecting her to call.

"Yes, I know, it's awful. He was like a son to me. I am going to miss him. Sure, sure, we've all traveled that road a million times, but you just never know... No, no, it's not going to be here. Risher near Lake George... Umm, no, I won't be home later, but I can talk to you tomorrow after the viewing... Okay, take care, Abby... You, too.'Bye," he said, wrapping up the unexpected call.

This time when he hung up the phone, he didn't gently place it in its cradle. His shaking hand dropped it to the floor. Bob picked up the phone and dialed the number that he knew all too well.

Chapter 16

Abby was putting together the rundown sheet for the six tonight. She would glance up every now and then to look at Paul. He was struggling today; it wasn't the best idea for him to come into work. He looked at the paper about the accident and threw it away. Dave suggested that he take a few days off, but Paul said he would be okay. From the minute he walked through the door, he was on the phone, scribbling in his reporter's book. His inviting grin didn't appear at all today. After thumbing through the phone book and jotting down something in his notebook, he jumped up and grabbed his coat. Abby figured she should interject now.

"Are you going home?" she asked, hoping that he would heed everyone's advice.

"No, I'm working on something; I'll be back later. I have a live shot for the six anyway," he said with one foot out the door.

"We could always put someone else on that story."

"I'll be back later," he repeated, ending the conversation.

Abby didn't even get a chance to ask how he was holding up.

Dave walked over to Abby's desk.

"Boy, I'm surprised he is here today. You can't tell him to go home, though. How's he doing anyway?" he asked.

She didn't want to get into it and told him he was handling it well.

"That's good. Here's that heart health package. It's edited already."

"Thanks. Do you know where Paul was going?" she asked, without sounding too curious.

"He said he'll be back. You can call or page him if anyone is looking for him."

Abby wondered why Paul didn't give her this information before he left.

Chapter 17

The morning of the viewing, Abby woke early, although she wasn't sure why since she was on the phone with Paul for the majority of the evening. She had ended their conversation by telling him she would see him at the service.

Her bedroom was cold, so she kept her comforter wrapped around her as she walked to the window. The weather outside was bleak. The sky was gray and it looked cold. It, too, was in mourning. It was almost March, but no signs of approaching spring.

Abby debated whether or not she should get motivated or go back to bed. She told Dave this would be one of her days off, and he didn't mind. She figured today would be a long day. There was only one viewing scheduled, but she knew how emotionally draining the few hours would be.

The comforter swooshed as she dragged it across the floor and curled back up into bed. Just as she wondered if she would be able to fall back to sleep, she closed her eyes and it came quite effortlessly.

* * * *

There was a slight shuffling sound coming from the living room that startled Abby out of her slumber. She wasn't sure if the sound was coming from outside the house or inside. Her heart pounded in her chest, partially from being awaken suddenly and partially from not knowing the origin of the noise.

She discarded the blanket that she was tangled in and stood by her bedroom door. The hardwood flooring that she loved answered her every step with a groaning creak. She figured it was stupid to be afraid in her own house and she marched into her kitchen, only to hear the steady hum of her refrigerator. She flipped on the lights. A bright, white envelope was peeking out from underneath her door. She hoped the person that left it there wasn't waiting on the other side. She walked over and picked it up, then peered out the peek hole. The envelope was light and felt like nothing was in it. She slid her finger under the unsealed flap. Inside was tucked a small piece of paper with words neatly centered. The bold letters grabbed her attention and sent her mind spinning.

Without thinking twice, she flung the door open and headed to the main entrance. She squinted when she stepped onto the doorstop. Even though the day wasn't flooded with sunlight, the brightness of the new morning caused her eyes to adjust. She didn't see anyone standing around or any odd cars. Whoever left this message for Abby was long gone, or watching from somewhere unseen.

With that idea, she stepped back into the dimly lit outside corridor and read the note over and over.

Ignore the past; concern yourself with your future.

Chapter 18

The bleak afternoon stayed consistent with the morning. Abby couldn't wait for the weather to break. The ever present cold temperatures were exaggerated by the whipping wind.

Abby wanted so badly to tell Paul about the note that she found. As she drove to the funeral home, she thought it was best that she waited. Now was the time to grieve, not to worry about what she had found. For all she knew, it would be written off as nothing serious in everyone else's mind. She definitely didn't see it that way.

As she followed the rural road towards town, she noticed the snow on the side of the pavement. She knew how treacherous the roads could get in the mountains, but she also knew it wasn't Jeremy's first time attempting to journey them. Regardless, the viewing was going to be arduous for Paul. She wondered if he realized how trying it would be.

Abby pulled up in front of the Risher Funeral Home. While most of these structures were designed to look stately but unassuming, this one looked like a ranch style home straight from the 1950s. It loomed before her, sprawled out as unwelcoming as a new school on the first day. The parking lot was crowded, and she was waved past the regular lot to the dirt area beside the house. She scoured the crowd of people outside for a familiar face, but did not find one. She had on a long black skirt with a simple black sweater. She looked down at her feet as she walked towards the door and realized that she may have overdone it. She always thought that it was customary to wear all black to viewings and funerals, but she noticed that some of the others were in colors not so dreary.

A thin man with a face too shiny and glasses too large nodded to Abby as she walked into the door. The overwhelming fragrance of carnations and roses, plus a myriad of different flowers greeted her as soon as she entered the funeral parlor. The beauty that they represented also provided the feeling of fear and trepidation in such a setting. The room was set up with row upon row of chairs facing the casket. Abby couldn't see it exactly, but knew that past the sea of people, Jeremy's body lay between the two large brass floor lamps that were spewing bright light onto the ceiling above. She could see the source of her repulsion peeking their petals and leaves out above the people's heads. She walked deeper into the room, acknowledging others as she proceeded. She wasn't sure if these people were his family or friends, but she still did not find Paul or anyone else recognizable. As she drew closer, the smell became stronger. The sickening floral essence mixed with several different perfumes worn too heavily and the unmistakable odor of people nervous with perspiration cramped into a small room with low ceilings was making Abby ill. She tried to push through the crowd, but her purse held her back. She turned to see what it was caught on when she saw him.

"Here, let me help." Paul came up behind her and unhooked her handbag from the loop of a chair. He followed protocol and was dressed in a black suit. His crisp, white shirt was divided by a deep burgundy tie. She couldn't make out what his cuff links were, but she knew that he looked striking.

"Hey, thanks. How are you?" she whispered. Abby waited until the viewing hours were half over to arrive. She hated when people walked in immediately after the family was first shown the body. She knew by now Paul would be a little more at ease standing in this dreaded room, but not making the situation itself all that easier.

Paul placed his hand on her waist and guided her towards the front. "I saw you come in but I couldn't make it to the back of the room fast enough. Thanks for coming, Ab. I will walk up with you," he said.

Abby was trying to stall, but he ushered her to the front. What she saw lying before her made her gasp. She waited for the few people in front of her to pay their respects and walk over to the family. She bit the inside of her mouth and tried to place her mind elsewhere. She watched as a woman dressed in brown leaned in to embrace a woman that must have been Jeremy's mother. Abby stood in front of the casket and lowered her head in prayer, but the only thing going through her mind was how bad the accident must have been in order for them not to be able to have an open casket viewing. The ebony coffin was flanked by several groups of the unbearable flowers, their colors meshing together as her eyes filled with tears. She tried not to blink, but she could not prevent the small streams running down each cheek. She felt light-headed and warm and did not want to be in this room. A picture of Jeremy that was taken on a fall day a few years ago sat atop the casket. In it, Jeremy was stooping down with his arms around his golden retriever. The smile on his face portrayed his love for life. Abby didn't even look at the two poster boards that were on the easel situated amongst the arrangements; she knew they would consist of the storyline of Jeremy's life. She stepped back from the coffin and waited for Paul to make the introductions.

"Mrs. Greish, Mr. Greish, this is my friend Abby. And this is Jeremy's sister," he said, acknowledging a slight girl who looked like she was barely old enough to drive and whose face was red and sobbing, continuous.

The girl muttered something that resembled "thanks for coming" then plopped back down in the chair. Her mother sat next to her, rubbing her back.

"Thank you, Abby, for coming," Jeremy's father said.

"I'm so sorry. I just met Jeremy within the past few months and he really was a great person. He is going to be missed." She never knew the right words to say at times like these. She also knew from her experience with her mom and with Becca that few consoling sentences were remembered. Mr. Greish thanked her all the same.

Without making this more difficult than it was, she moved on, slightly touching Mrs. Greish's shoulder and her daughter's. *Oh, how they were hurting*, she thought to herself. Abby knew the pain they were going through; she just hoped this didn't happen because she appeared in Jeremy's life. This made the tears unstoppable as she pushed her way to the back of the room.

Paul was on her heels. "I wasn't sure if I told you about the closed casket or not," he said. "The accident was so traumatic…" He stopped at that.

Abby didn't need to hear anymore. She was very shocked by the picture on the casket. For as gruesome as it seems, seeing the deceased usually helped with the realization that they were gone. Abby thought that seeing only the picture of Jeremy as happy as he was only made it seem like he just didn't show up here today.

"Yeah, I think you mentioned something, but it was still hard." She looked at Paul's face and saw the sorrow in his eyes. He looked tired, but he was still holding up better than the others sitting in the ugly, upholstered chairs at the front of the room. She knew that Paul's strength was helping the Greish family. She didn't want to take him away; this wasn't about her.

"Go back with them," she urged as she grabbed his hand.

He squeezed her palm and pulled her close to him. He whispered into her hair then held her shoulders. "Thanks again for being here, I mean it. This is hard for me, but when I saw you show up through that door, it was my only source of relief this entire day. I will call you tonight." He kissed her on the cheek and flashed one more smile before straightening his tie and heading back to console his best friend's family.

Abby sat down in the very back of the room and watched as Paul sat next to Jeremy's little sister and put his arm around her shoulder, bringing her head against him. She knew she must have felt some relief. Abby sat there for a while thinking about Jeremy, and also about her mom and Becca, and how much she missed all of them.

She heard someone talking by the front door and looked up.

"Yes, he worked with me for quite some time. What a great kid." Then there was a pause. "I am going to miss him," the man said, followed by sniffling.

"Well, again, I'm sorry, Mr. Franklin," another man said.

Abby stopped everything she was thinking. That name was the only thing that resonated in her head. She forgot that she told him she would speak to him. She watched as he sat down in one of the chairs, sighing and pushing the palm of his hands onto the top of his legs. He sat with his hands folded, letting them hang between his knees. The filtered light gleamed off the top of his balding head. His hair was fashioned in a poor comb-over style that he reached up to fix. His face was moon shaped, with a perfectly centered, turned-down mustache. A slight beading of sweat graced his brow as he toggled back and forth from staring at the floor to his hands. Abby wasn't sure this was the right time to talk to him.

A few minutes later, he walked outside. Abby checked to see if Paul was watching her. When she noticed that his back was to her, she followed Mr. Franklin out the door, hoping that he did not leave.

"Mr. Franklin?" she asked, trying to sound as sympathetic as possible. She wanted to feel him out first, before she got into too many questions. "Hi, I'm Abby. We spoke earlier?"

"Hi, Abby. Yes we did. What was it you said you needed?" he asked.

Abby didn't want to delve directly into the conversation that she was leaning towards. She averted her main agenda for now. "I just wanted to say that I am so sorry about Jeremy. I heard that you were close with him after working together for several years. Paul said you were good to him. This must be hard for you."

Bob Franklin shifted from foot to foot, keeping his arms folded. He stared off into the distance, not looking directly at Abby. She realized that this was upsetting him and she wasn't sure if this was the right time to bring this up. At this point, Bob still had sweat streaming down his face, despite the fact that it had to be only thirty degrees out.

"Are you okay?" she asked.

"I'm...okay, I guess. I know why you are here, Abby. Why don't you just ask me what it is that you want?" He did not waste any time.

"If you are too upset, it could wait," she lied.

"No, we can talk now. Do you want to go back inside? We can sit over by the desk where they hand out the prayer cards. Mr. Risher won't have a problem with that."

They walked back into the funeral home and stepped into the room on the left. After a few words exchanged between the two funeral directors, Bob motioned for Abby to come sit by the roll top desk. She sat in a hard wooden chair with its unforgiving back. She leaned forward to perch on the end. The lights were dimmed low in this room, but she could feel heat from the glowing desk lamp that was turned towards her face. Bob must have noticed this, so he reached over to turn it away.

"I know all about the project you and Paul are working on. And I know that this leads you back to Becca and that Jeremy told you some things," he said. "I want to set something straight right now. Almost twelve years ago when your friend died and she was brought to my funeral home, she overdosed on pills. As far as I was concerned and according to the coroner's report, she committed suicide. You know that," he whispered.

This sudden change of subject made Abby shift in her seat.

"Jeremy brought up all of those questions and theories right off the bat, and I will admit, I wrote it off as an overeager kid trying to play super sleuth. Then as years went by, I found out some of the details. I have to admit that I had some doubt in my mind. It was a stretch, but the doubt was there," he continued then paused.

"What details, Mr. Franklin?" she asked.

"The fact the Jonathan and Theresa mentioned Becca's father and how he tried repeatedly to swindle money from her estate after her death. It just made me think. I never mentioned anything to Jeremy because I knew where he would go with it. Plus, there was just too much involved to resurface something. It would have been too hard for the Rices to have to deal with something like that."

"So wait, you both had doubt, but you just let it go? Isn't that illegal? And why were you talking to the Rices about this anyway?" she questioned, trying not to sound too argumentative.

Mr. Franklin sat upright in his chair, straightening his tie. "Look, Abby, I don't have to tell you any of this. I am not the bad guy here. I don't even know if there is a bad guy, to tell you the truth. I am just telling you that Colin Parsons was up to no good. Maybe I should have mentioned something about the whole thing, but we have no proof. Again, it would be a tragedy to have to unearth this entire situation again." He was getting frustrated, and Abby knew that this question and answer session was going to come to a close.

"I'm sorry. I don't mean to upset you. I'm just trying to do some research," she said.

"Well, what I wanted to tell you was that a few days before Jeremy died, I received a phone call at the funeral home. It was someone returning Jeremy's call, but he wasn't around. It didn't sound like anyone I recognized, and he wouldn't leave a message. When I told Jeremy about it, he just blew it off."

"What does that have to do with anything?"

He leaned close to her. "I don't know what happened to Becca. Personally, and it's probably hard for you to hear, I think she killed herself, but if, one day, someone told me otherwise, I wouldn't be totally blown out of the water. I know what Jeremy always thought all of these years and I am sure it played on his mind. When you brought it up, it was pulled off of the back burner again. The problem is, whether or not Colin had anything to do with his daughter's death is probably not the issue; the part about him trying to swindle money is. That could have happened either way," he explained. "I think when Jeremy started poking around again, which I know he was doing, someone didn't like it. Even if a person didn't kill someone, they could still go to prison for trying to swindle an estate. I am as sure about Jeremy's accident being just that as Becca's suicide. That is what I am having a hard time with," he said.

He lowered his head and looked like he was ready to cry. Abby took this as her cue to go.

"Thanks, Mr. Franklin, for talking with me. I will call you if I hear anything else," she said, standing up.

"Be careful, Abby, both you and Paul. You have as much information as Jeremy did."

"I realize that," she said, as she was reminded of her note when she reached into her pocket. She now had to interpret the mixed signals she just received.

Chapter 19

Theresa Rice picked up some of the boxes that were on the twin bed and relocated them into the hallway. It was time to clean this room out. They both agreed they would use it for a reading room, but not only did they not get around to the remodeling, it became a bigger and bigger storage area whenever they would find something they didn't know what to do with. Not like the house wasn't big enough to store things; this room was just for odds and ends. Theresa loved this house. She knew how much Jonathan adored it while he was growing up and loved keeping it in the family. There was still so much to be done to get it to their liking, but in the meantime, most people that visited remarked how amazing it looked. Theresa was proud of her decorating, even though sometimes her taste got a little too expensive. Jonathan had a flair for style, which made it easy to persuade him. Her daily job as a sales manager brought on a lot of stress in her life, and decorating allowed her to express more creativity.

She sat on the bed and dusted off some old albums that Jonathan refused to part with. She remembered the time when they were newly married. She and Jonathan constantly traveled and spent money as quickly as they earned it. When Becca entered their lives, it changed everything.

Theresa stooped down to pick up one of the boxes that she placed outside the room. The sunlight bathed the faded hardwood and made it obvious that this room had not been touched for years. Dust particles danced in the warm beams focused on the floor. Theresa juggled the box and tried to get a better grip. The contents were heavier than Theresa thought. She dropped the cardboard container and created a gray cloud in front of her face.

She rummaged through the tablets and papers on the top of the box and found a marble-based trophy. Its base felt cool as Theresa ran her hand over the swirled stone. A cheap, plastic figure was anchored in the top. Theresa wiped away the dust to read the inscription scrawled into the plaque. It was for a science fair that Becca took first place in when she was in second grade. Theresa didn't know her then, but when Becca moved into their home, she brought her entire life with her in a few containers. Small boxes holding trinkets and several notebooks filled out the rest of the contents.

Theresa headed downstairs and had managed to carry the box into the foyer when the phone rang. She hurried to answer the phone and sat down when she realized it was a friend she hadn't heard from in a while. She wiped her dusty hands on her jeans and her brow on her sleeve. As the caller droned on and on, she was thankful when there was a knock at the door.

"I'll have to call you back; someone is here," Theresa said. She was glad to get off the phone after a thirty minute play by play of her friend's latest dating drama. She looked in the mirror and pushed her hair away from her forehead; that was the most she could do before answering the door. "Oh, hi, Abby, Paul," she said after opening the door. "Come in. Jonathan isn't home yet, but you're welcome to stay."

"We are not bothering you, are we?" Paul asked. He looked at Theresa and noticed her jeans had dirt on the legs and a charcoal smudge was smeared across her cheek.

"Oh, no," she said, patting herself down and turning to study herself in the mirror again. "I was just cleaning upstairs and getting rid of old things. You can't imagine how much junk you can accumulate in a few years. You know what, I'll be right back. Let me just wash some of this dirt off," she said as she turned to run up the stairs.

Abby and Paul remained in the foyer

"I'm sorry, Paul. You probably don't want to be here. We will only stay for a few minutes. You said you didn't mind, right? I mean, if you want to leave now, we can," Abby whispered. She kept her eyes focused on the stairs, awaiting Theresa's return.

"I told you I didn't mind stopping over for a little while. Relax," he said.

Abby mentioned dropping by since it was on their way home. Considering there was only one viewing and it was so early, she figured she would ask Paul if he would accompany her. She wasn't even sure if anyone was home, but she wanted to ask the Rices a few questions. Abby looked around the foyer again, admiring the stately beauty of the home. That was when she noticed the box.

"Paul, look," she said, not taking her eyes off of what was in front of her.

"Yeah, it looks like a box of old stuff."

Abby was already crouching down, picking things up, when she saw the tablet. The blue notebook had a large daisy sticker on the cover. She remembered that Becca kept a tablet on her dresser. Abby continuously pressed Becca to reveal the contents of her journal, but Becca always said it was her secret diary. It didn't have a lock and key, but Abby honored Becca's wishes and never pried. She instantly knew that the tablet with the copper-ringed coil and telltale sticker was Becca's.

"I know that is Becca's," Abby whispered to Paul. "I wonder if they would let me take it home to read. It's giving me goose bumps just thinking about it. I hope Theresa wasn't planning on throwing all of this stuff out." Abby continued her search through the dusty box.

She jumped when Theresa walked back in. "Oh, I'm sorry, I just noticed some of Becca's things here and I couldn't help but look," Abby said, slightly embarrassed.

Theresa didn't seem upset. "I was cleaning upstairs and I came across some of her belongings. I thought we had all of that packed away, but there were still a few things around. I was in the process of taking them downstairs before you came over."

"The thing that caught my eye was Becca's diary. I recognized it by that big daisy on the front. If you don't mind, I would like to take that home for a few days. It would bring back some old memories," Abby said, walking over to pick it up.

Theresa's hand stopped her. "I hate to do this, but I'm going to have to say no. I mean, I would like to check with Jonathan first. He gets weird about that stuff. The whole situation still gets him upset. Let me run it by him. I'm sure he won't mind, but I should have his permission," Theresa said. She stood in front of the box and denied Abby any further access. "Why don't you both come in and sit down?"

"Yeah, sure," Abby said. She was a little surprised by Theresa's response. She didn't think it was that big of a deal. Abby tried to change this uncomfortable subject as soon as possible. "We won't keep you. I just wanted to show you something."

As they walked into the living room, Theresa mentioned Jeremy's tragic accident. Abby thought it was thoughtful of her to offer her condolences. She was surprised that she heard about it. But of all people, Abby should know that news spreads fast in this town and that everyone knows everything.

"How is Jeremy's family holding up?" Theresa asked, directing it towards Paul.

"Okay, I guess. As good as they could be in a time like this," he said.

Abby knew that Paul didn't want to talk about Jeremy's death, and Theresa sensed it as well.

"Well, I just want you to know I'm very sorry to hear about it," she said. She sat on one of the couches and pulled one leg underneath her.

Abby studied her face and wondered how her hair would look falling around it. Every time Abby saw her, Theresa had her hair pulled back very tight in a neat ponytail. She wondered if she ever truly relaxed. The few times she met with her lately, Theresa was always well dressed. Today, since Theresa was cleaning, she was somewhat dressed down, but still looked together. This thin, well-polished woman had one noticeable flaw: she was anxious. From the moment Abby and Paul walked into the house, Theresa could not remain still. She constantly shifted from foot to foot from the time they sat on the couch.

The letter was in Abby's pocket. She reached in to reassure herself that it was there. The note was the reason Paul agreed to go with her. He didn't have much to say about the enclosed message, but he was concerned. The past two days drained him, and Abby didn't think he had the energy to put much thought into anything. She didn't push the issue that maybe Jeremy's accident wasn't just that, but she was sure Paul got that vibe from her. He wouldn't have agreed to come with her otherwise.

Theresa tucked a stray strand of hair behind her ear and leaned forward with her elbows resting on her knees, hands clasped. She waited to see what it was now that Abby had brought. Without another word, Abby handed her the letter. She watched for her expression. Theresa unfolded the paper and smoothed it on her leg. She must have been reading it over a few times, since she did not immediately look up. When she did, she looked at Abby.

"So what do you think this means?" she asked.

"I have been thinking about what you said the other day about Colin. If for some reason Becca did not commit suicide but was murdered, and the murderer thought that it would never be revealed, don't you think he might be cautious if he discovered that people were digging up information?"

Theresa sat upright on the couch now. "Abby, I told you that story in confidence, and it is just my opinion. I have no proof of anything. I just said if anyone was to blame, it would make sense to point a finger at Colin." Her pale skin was now flushed with two red streaks under each cheekbone. She was unmistakably annoyed.

"I know, but with Jeremy's accident and now this letter, I think someone is trying to keep something quiet. In my opinion, I think Jeremy knew too much about Becca's death. It's odd that for the first time in years, he brings information to light and then dies in a car accident. Afterwards, I get that letter," she said, pointing to the white sheet still clenched in Theresa's hand.

Theresa placed the letter on the table between them. "Okay, okay, wait a minute. You have all of these grandiose ideas and theories and then someone spooks you with a letter. Did you ever think that maybe it has something to do with the Jensen suicide? Maybe people are upset about the series you are working on. This topic you are dealing with really hits home, and you did the coverage on the Jensen girl so damn fast. Maybe people just don't like it, Abby. I thought talking to that poor girl's mother was a little premature myself," she said, her face now bright red.

"I don't think Abby is asking your opinion on what we do at work, Theresa," Paul interjected. This was the first time that he entered this conversation, taking Abby's side.

"Well, then, what is it that you want from me?" she asked, her voice filled with sarcasm.

"We just need your help with all of the information you could supply us with about Colin. I need to know the last time you had contact with him, what you know about his family, and so forth. I think we should ask Jonathan for his information on this matter as well."

Theresa stood up and walked towards the archway. "Good, that's perfect. Bring up all of these crazy ideas then push my husband for information and make him revisit such a dark time from his past. That makes sense."

Abby and Paul stood up at the same time.

"You know what, Theresa, maybe we shouldn't have stopped by and bothered you. We should just do this on our own," Abby said, turning back to pick up her letter.

They didn't make any additional agreements to talk about the situation. Abby doubted that Theresa would let her bring this up to Jonathan. She felt her energies and research were best applied elsewhere.

She looked down at the box one last time and pondered over the idea to pick up the diary and take it. Theresa must have read her mind. She again acted as a blockade and separated Abby and the dusty box on the floor. There was no further explanation.

"Good night," was all Theresa said before closing the door.

Abby and Paul walked down the porch steps and got into the car. Abby couldn't see her face, but the sliver of light that shone through the small area between the curtain and doorframe proved that Theresa was watching them leave.

"Abby, before you even ask, no, I don't know why she is so dead set against helping us. Maybe they are just that troubled by the whole thing. Maybe they feel guilty about Becca's death because they weren't there to protect her no matter what the cause. Or maybe Theresa is just a bitch," Paul said.

Abby chuckled at this last comment and realized that this was the first time she laughed in days. They both broke into hysterics.

"I'm sorry, I haven't laughed for quite some time," Paul said, wiping away tears of laughter from his eyes.

It was good to see him happy. Abby knew how hard it was for Paul to be dealing with all of this. They didn't even go through Jeremy's funeral yet, and Abby was dragging Paul around, investigating her problems. She respected the fact that he didn't want to talk about this.

"Do you want to catch a movie or get something to eat?" she suggested. "I'm hungry now, but we can get some snacks at the movies and make it in time for an earlier show. If you don't want to, I'll understand. I just thought it might be good to help get your mind off of things."

Paul paused for a second and then smiled. "A movie sounds like a good idea," he said, already driving in that direction.

They didn't speak the rest of the way to the theater. Abby was just happy to get his mind off of Jeremy. She wasn't pleased about how things went at the Rices.

They made it to the movie a few minutes before it started. Normally, she wouldn't agree to watch one of these teen spoof movies, and neither would Paul, but it seemed like the most lighthearted choice. Abby found two seats while Paul went to get popcorn. She shed her coat and looked around at the few other people in the theater. The lights were still on, but dimmed enough to keep some things in the dark. The theater was old, but still had a neat feeling about it. Abby put her hand on the fabric that covered the chair. The worn nylon felt smooth. Her feet made a quiet sticking sound as she tapped them on the floor. But she couldn't think of a better place to get away from everything. Abby always loved the movies, and once the lights went out and the screen lit up, she could rest assured that her troubles would be out of her mind for at least two hours. The calmness, the smell of buttered popcorn, and the quiet hiss of the projector were always an instant retreat for Abby.

Just as the lights were dimming, Paul returned, juggling two different boxes of candy, a jumbo tub of popcorn, and two sodas.

"Good," she whispered. "We won't have to get something to eat later." She grabbed some of the concessions from him as he sat down next to her.

"I know you're hungry, but this should tide us over," he said.

She smiled and popped a few pieces of popcorn into her mouth. She sunk down into the comfortable chair and they were now enveloped in darkness. The first credits rolled in front of them and Abby's cares rolled off the screen with them as she leaned against Paul.

Chapter 20

Abby didn't want to get out of bed. The thought of attending a funeral made it even harder. She pressed against the window. Its icy chill felt refreshing against her forehead. If the cold glass didn't remind her that winter was wrapping up, the golden rays and brightness would have tricked her into thinking spring already arrived. It helped some that the day was cheerful, but she knew it wouldn't matter in a few hours.

She walked over to her dresser and ran her finger along the edge, accumulating a decent amount of dust. She should probably do some heavy spring-cleaning. She flicked the gray particles off the tip of her finger. They landed on the folded paper in the center of her dresser. The note. She didn't forget about it, she just decided to prioritize things now, with Paul's situation coming first. She promised herself that the meaning behind the note from the unknown author would be discovered next.

By the time she got dressed, she realized she did not have enough time for breakfast. A can of orange juice and a shortbread cookie would have to do for now.

She looked herself over in her full-length mirror and thought she was wearing too much black today. Since she knew she couldn't be late, she grabbed a strand of fake pearls and tried to arrange them on her neckline. Knowing that she was not a pearl person, she tossed them aside and ran out the door.

* * * *

The funeral home was packed as expected. It took forever to get everyone in the procession line. She saw Paul, but he was near the Greish family, so she didn't want to bother him.

The early morning hours did not allow for the heat to fully kick on in the funeral home. It wasn't cold, but it wasn't comfortable. She kept her coat on, and this solved the dress dilemma.

The flowers were so overpowering at this point that she couldn't wait to leave the funeral home. The air was filled with the pungent odor of death. Abby couldn't pinpoint it, but the combination of different scents nauseated her.

She looked at her watch and then around the room to see how many people still had to file out. It was odd not having someone to go with. She would drive her own car and didn't even think of asking anyone else to accompany her. She didn't really have anyone else. Paul was going to be a pallbearer, she didn't see Bob Franklin, and she didn't feel comfortable tagging along with Jeremy's family.

The church bells tolled and the lights were dimmed. The silence that surrounded her was pierced by the occasional sob and sniffling. Abby chose not to look at the family as they filtered in. She refused to watch the coffin as it was brought down the aisle. She tried not to pay attention to much of what was going on. In her mind, if she didn't think about it, she wouldn't break down. She was afraid of breaking down. She contemplated her own religious status. She had been raised Catholic, and her family rarely missed a mass when she was growing up. Ever since her mom died, she didn't find as much time for church. She was lucky to be seen on Christmas and Easter. Her dad always hounded her to start going again. Today, sitting here thinking about everything, she vowed she would.

Abby was startled by someone sliding into the pew next to her.

"Hi, Abby," he said.

"Mr. Franklin," she said and nodded.

She rose with the rest of the congregation. He missed the morning service, and now he was late for the mass. Above all, he knew this drill better than anyone. Now Abby's wish to be with someone today changed; she wished she was sitting by herself.

The remainder of the service found Bob Franklin silent. He kept his head down most of the time, fighting back tears. Abby stared ahead.

As they exited the church, Paul caught her glance once or twice. She felt a bit selfish. She was very upset, but it wasn't just because of Jeremy. It brought back sad thoughts of her mom and Becca. Her tears fell for many reasons.

* * * *

The graveside service was very emotional. Mrs. Greish slumped into the chair as she sat in front of her son's coffin. She leaned on her husband's shoulder and dropped the folded tissues from her lap. Someone ran over with smelling salts and tried to bring her around. The sorrow she was enduring brought everyone to tears.

The congregation grew silent, except for the whisper of unsuccessfully muffled sobs. Abby pulled her coat tightly around herself and tried to prevent her heels from sinking too deep into the mud.

At the end of the service, Paul walked over to Abby and hugged her. He embraced her with such strength that she couldn't even lift her arms to return the emotion. She felt his body shake and knew it hit him. This was the final stage and the last time with his friend. Paul lifted his head and revealed swollen, red eyes that he wiped at incessantly.

"I know how you feel, and it will get easier," she said.

Paul looked at the gravesite and watched as the cemetery maintenance crew started to prepare the vault and ready Jeremy's casket to be lowered into its final resting place. Paul turned away. Abby couldn't watch either. He put his arm around her and they walked towards her car.

"Thanks for everything, Abby."

That was all he said as she drove him back to the funeral home to get his car. He didn't need to say anything else. She knew he couldn't. He waved as he jogged over to his car, his wool coat tails flapping behind him. His wavy hair slicked with gel made him look sharp, but there was nothing that could hide the sadness in his face. Abby knew exactly how he felt.

When she returned home, Abby walked through her living room without bothering to take her coat off. She went straight to her window and sat down. Outside, the sun glittered off of the traces of melting snow. Spring was near and everything was wet and muddy now. This was the transition everyone had to go through to reach something brighter. She thought of Jeremy's life cut short. The tears flowed heavy now with no signs of stopping. She muffled her cry in her coat sleeve. The harsh wool irritated her nose as she wiped her face. She could no longer avoid breaking down.

Chapter 21

Paul walked into the station and tried to get his mind on business as usual. However, Dave was lingering near his desk. "What's up, Dave?" he asked without lifting his head. He went right to his email without pausing for his normal morning chatter.

"Stop in my office when you settle in," Dave said.

Great, Paul thought. *Today was supposed to be a day to coast by and even cut out early.*

He followed Dave into the small, cluttered office. Papers, books, and magazines were spilling off of the small desk. Paul studied the pictures of Dave and people he considered famous that he had the chance to interview. He sensed that his boss was unsure how to break into this conversation.

"So, how are you holding up?" Dave eventually asked. He sounded as sincere as he could.

"Well, it's not easy, but I'll manage. What did you need?" Paul was trying to make this meeting as brief as possible.

"I need to talk to you and Abby about the series you are working on. The promotions department has been scheduling your promo. I know you did the first installment, but we need to follow up soon. I don't want to wait until May sweeps, and we actually got a few calls from people asking when we were going to do the special." Dave stared intently at the eraser on his pencil and tapped it against the desk.

Paul doubted that he got any calls inquiring about their little story, but he humored Dave, although he actually found it a little inconsiderate for Dave to be bringing this up now. He reassured him that he would talk to Abby as soon as she came in and they would wrap up the next part.

"We can run over today and get some footage. We interviewed Mrs. Jensen last time, but we didn't get any video. Could someone help with the other story I was scheduled to do?" he asked, with one foot out the office door.

"I'll put James on that. He could shoot and do voice over and then put the package together for tonight. Just see what you guys can get done. Let me know if you need anything, okay?" he finished.

Paul liked how he tried to throw one more sympathetic touch in. "Thanks, I'll be okay," he responded.

Abby walked in and Paul didn't hesitate to fill her in. He didn't want her feeling sorry for him, so he jumped right into it.

"Hey, I just talked to Dave and we need to do something about our story," he said.

Abby set her stuff down and grabbed last night's rundowns from her inbox. "How are you, first?"

"I'm okay; I just need to get my mind off of the whole situation."

Abby furrowed her brow and pursed her lips. She looked at the paper, purposely avoiding Paul.

He hadn't meant to offend her. "I appreciate that you're concerned about me, but really, I am okay." He touched her arm and drew a warmer response. She gave him one of her inviting smirks that turned into a smile. Her hair was still damp, and she smelled of perfumed soap and citrus. She made him feel at ease.

"Okay, so what's up?" she inquired, realizing that it was okay to change the subject now.

"The series we've been working on. Dave wants something together to air soon. I think he is a little disappointed that we don't have material air-ready right now. I told him we will change that. We have our work cut out for us. Can you stay later tonight to edit?"

"Yeah, sure," she said, but her mind was already elsewhere. Immediately, the wheels started turning in her head. She thought that whoever gave her that note would be waiting to see if they were going to continue with their research and series. This installment could draw that person out. The idea both scared and excited Abby.

"Just to prepare you: Nancy Drew is back," she said, hoping Paul would find it amusing.

He chimed in immediately, "I figured as much. And I bet that I can almost read your mind as to where this is going. You think if we air the Jensen story, make reference to Becca, and throw a few more things into it that we will get someone's attention, right?"

He was definitely on the same page. She wondered if he felt as strongly about the entire situation.

"Paul, I'm doing this story because it's my job. I'm doing it because it will look great on my résumé. But you have to understand that I have other ties to this as well. If we could help someone else, that will be great. If we could help ourselves out, that would be even better." Abby knew that sounded selfish, but Paul was just as involved in this now as she was. "I'll call Mrs. Jensen right now. I have to get some follow up information and I would like to explain a few things."

"Ab, you don't have to do that. I'm sure—"

"No, I want her to know why I was so upset. I want her to know that I understand. I do understand, Paul." Abby stared at Paul and wanted him to know that she did understand. She knew what he was going through. She knew what Mrs. Jensen was dealing with, too.

Her look must have reassured him. Paul walked away from her desk and yelled back over his shoulder. "After we finish tonight, plan on getting something to eat with me," he said.

Abby smiled and was happy that he didn't give her the chance to turn down the invitation. She wouldn't have anyway.

* * * *

"Hi, Mrs. Jensen, thanks for letting me drop by again," Abby said, emphasizing her last word. As she walked into the house, she felt more confident this time. The atmosphere was the same. The pictures of Christa surrounded her and the quietness of the house was interrupted only by the repetition of the grandfather clock in the hall. Last time she was here, she could hear her heart and was sure everyone else could, too.

"How are you, Abby? I'm sorry that I upset you so much last time," Mrs. Jensen said, reaching out to touch Abby's hand.

Abby felt guilty. "No, it's me that should be sorry. We shouldn't have been here that soon after Christa's death, and I just wasn't prepared. I wanted to explain myself."

"No need, no need," Mrs. Jensen said, waving her hand.

Mrs. Jenson looked a little better than the last time they met, but Abby knew the game of acting composed around people during the day because life must go on. It was the night that people didn't see. They didn't hear the muffled cries into a pillow or see the reddened nose and irritated eyes from lack of sleep and a night full of sobbing. Imagination and sadness crept in with the dark, flooding thoughts and blocking all means of escape. Abby didn't want to bring this up.

"Don't apologize. I know what happened to Becca, dear. This is a small town, and when I found out, it all came back to me. I thank you for your understanding," she said.

Abby was stunned by this comment. She assumed Paul must have explained things to her, but wondered why he didn't say anything. She let Mrs. Jensen finish speaking.

They talked for over an hour, and at the end, Abby knew more about Christa. It felt good to talk about Becca, and they could both relate to their situations. Abby needed this final interview for her piece, but she also needed it for her peace of mind.

As she prepared to leave, Mrs. Jensen added something.

"Abby, Christa really was a sweet girl. She wasn't a bad person. I think the story you are doing is great, but don't make my little girl out to be a bad person. If this could help someone, I'm sure Christa would be happy," she said.

Abby reassured her it would be produced in good taste with the best intentions. She thanked her and headed back to the station. She didn't even mention her predicament. It wasn't fair to voice her concerns and problems. It was Mrs. Jensen who needed to talk and receive sympathy. Abby felt a little guilty that she went there for more than just that.

When she arrived back at the station, Paul was engrossed in his computer.

"I talked to Mrs. Jensen, and it went fairly well. She was upset, but she is happy that we are doing this. How's your stuff going?" she inquired as she threw her coat on the chair.

"Everything is going well. I talked to Children and Youth, the police department, and the hospital. They gave me some numbers and stats to work with. It will fit in nicely. How did you, yourself, make out?" When he asked her this question, he stopped typing for a minute.

"Oh, I'm fine. It felt good to talk. I made out a lot better than last time. So what do we have to work on first?"

"Do you want to try editing together some of that file footage that we have for the background piece?"

"Wow, you're going to trust the lowly assignment editor to do her own editing? And what about the line up for the eleven?"

"Just get in there, already. As for tonight, Dave has us covered."

Abby walked back into the edit bay that consisted of a table with two decks and monitors and an old beat up chair. She grabbed the footage tapes and started piecing things together. Some of the information was just that. Abby had been exposed to elements of suicide and different theories for quite some time. Everyone else needed as much information as possible. Abby scanned the footage, looking for the perfect material. She hadn't edited for a while, but after an hour, the skill came back to her. After many hours of tedious searching, she felt a presence behind her.

"Hotshot," Paul said as he leaned over her shoulder, looking at the screens. His breath smelled of spearmint and there was still a trace of the ever-present spicy cologne. He placed his hands on her shoulders and gave them a big squeeze. "Aren't you ready to call it a night yet?"

Abby didn't realize how many hours she had been working. Her growling stomach also reminded her of their other plans: Dinner.

"I guess I could finish polishing tomorrow. What about the part about getting something to eat?" she asked.

"We have to be back in here in a few hours, but sure, a promise is a promise," he said.

They took separate cars and met in the barren diner's parking lot. She really was pushing herself to stay awake, but it would be worth it to do so.

* * * *

That night, however, Abby barely slept. She knew she had to be at work in a few hours so she figured she may as well stay up. It excited her that they would get the chance to show Dave what they produced, and she hoped it would lead to an earlier airing than planned. Abby knew Paul was eager to get it done as well, but his main objective wasn't the same as hers. She sensed that he was starting to tune in to some of her points of view.

She looked outside just as daylight started to peek through the murky sky. For being up so early with little sleep, she figured she must still be running on adrenalin. She rummaged through her closet for her sneakers. They literally had to be dusted off. She couldn't remember the last time she laced them up. Her New Year's resolution to exercise more was pushed back by the weather. She hated gyms but loved the outdoors. It would be cold, but nice enough to walk outside with a few layers of clothes.

Abby headed to the path behind her house. Her heavy sweatshirt that covered a turtleneck and a t-shirt shielded her from the morning cold. Her oversized mittens and headband did the trick for the rest of her body, but her nose started running as she accustomed herself to the morning frost. Her energy was propelling her to run, but she knew that since she hadn't since last year, she would have to start out slow. During her college years, Abby ran every day. In the summer, she ran on numerous trails in the Adirondack Mountains. It gave her time to think and appreciate everything around her. Her dad tried to convince her several times that she should carry mace or some other defense item, but the majestic forest where they lived did not seem the least bit conducive to any crime.

She made her way to the dirt path that was still frozen this morning. Thankfully, it was so solid, or she would have been slopping around in mud. Abby pumped her arms as she tried to stop herself from breaking into a run. She knew her lungs would take a week or two of conditioning before she did that again.

After twenty minutes, Abby turned around and headed back. It felt good to be outside again. Her quickened breath and her damp headband reminded her how much she missed this.

Chapter 22

"So he liked it?" Abby asked Paul. She knew they would look at the piece before she came in, but that was okay. Normally, she would like to be part of the entire process, but this was okay. The sooner Dave looked at it, the better.

"He said we did a great job. It's going to air tonight. No need for further editing,"

She knew Paul was pleased with this. He was happy about Dave's approval and that it would enhance his experience level. Abby was just happy it was going to air tonight.

"In the six tonight?" she asked.

"Yep," he said, stacking folders on his desk. "We still have a ton of things to do today. I have to make a few follow ups."

The rest of the day flew by. Abby called her dad to tell him their series was airing and she told Mrs. Jensen to prepare her. Now all they had to do was wait.

Abby worked the teleprompter for the six and her heart raced when the anchor led into their package. It went by so fast, but it looked good. She hoped all the right people saw it.

At six-thirty, Paul walked into the control room.

"It looked good. It looked really good," he said. "Do you want to go celebrate your first big production?"

Abby knew that she should go home and sleep, but the adrenaline still kept her going. She could push it for a few more hours.

"Pizza and beer sounds like a plan, what do you think?" she asked.

"Let's go. Do you want to drive? My tire is a little low."

Before they left, they got a few calls from the Jensens and Children and Youth commending the way they handled the piece. Overall, it was well-received.

The pizza parlor wasn't very crowded, and Abby and Paul devoured two small pies and tossed back more than enough beer. After about two hours, Abby really started to slow down. She wasn't sure if it was the beer, sleep deprivation, or both. Regardless, they headed out.

"Would you mind driving back to get your car? I think I'm too tired to drive," she asked.

"Or it could be that you had more beer than pizza." He laughed, grabbing her keys.

"I did not," she said, swatting him on the arm. She didn't think she should drive, though.

Paul walked over to the driver's side door and studied the keys in his hand to see which one opened the Honda. When he looked up to ask Abby, he noticed it. The white paper was fluttering underneath the driver-side windshield wiper. He froze for a moment, but then thought it could just be someone placing flyers. Abby's eyes were focused on the paper. Paul knew there was no way to hide it from her. Before grabbing it, he tried to determine what it was. The lights bounced off the windshield and blinded his view. This obstruction forced him to reach out and find out.

"What is it Paul?" she asked. All laughter and humor that he had heard for the past two hours had left her voice.

He didn't answer her.

"Paul, what is it?"

He grabbed the unfolded paper that was placed face down and snapped the wiper back in place. He slowly turned it over, figuring he wasn't going to see Tommy's Pizza's latest specials.

"It's a note," he said without letting his eyes leave the paper.

"And?" Her eyes were wide and her voice got higher.

Paul folded the note and tucked it in his pocket. He looked around the car and over by the restaurant.

"Just get in the car." He whispered this over the roof to Abby. His hands pushed against the top of the door. He then pushed himself back and flung the door open. Abby did the same.

Once locked in the car, he knew there was no sense in keeping it from her. He took the paper out of his pocket and handed it to Abby. The inside of the car made Paul shiver and it smelled musty from the dampness. He watched her as she opened it. Her face stayed expressionless as she read the words in front of her.

More harm than good; quit while you're ahead.

"I think we should give this to the police," Paul said.

"Why? It's not a threat. Plus, if we get them involved, it will scare away who is doing this. An investigation like that wouldn't be kept quiet. Let's just wait."

"Doesn't this bother you?" he asked, motioning towards the wilted paper.

"I told you that I expected this. For some reason, what we are sharing with the public is really troubling someone. I don't think it's because they are upset about the topic of suicide. There is more to this, Paul," she said.

Abby hoped he wouldn't change his mind now and get the police involved. She knew in the back of her mind that they may have to be clued into this at some point, but she wasn't ready for that yet. Hopefully, her timing as to when that point was would be correct.

Chapter 23

Abby originally felt like receiving this letter would solve her problems. She had a looming suspicion what the outcome of airing the story would be, but not so soon.

She stopped at her dad's after work to clue him in as to what was going on. Abby felt that she owed that to him.

"So what do you think?" she asked after telling her story. Abby studied her dad's face and winced in anticipation of his response. She wanted to keep him out of this as much as possible because she knew he would worry.

Maybe it was his concern, but the furrows she saw in his face aged him greatly. The deep wrinkles in his face weren't necessarily from age, but from years of being in the sun. He always had a handsome glow about him and a warm smile that erased any signs of time. She was proud of her dad and knew it was hard for him. Abby tried to help out as much as she could after her mother died, but she was pretty proud of the way he handled everything. She knew he still missed her mom; Abby missed her greatly, too. Every time she accomplished something at work or had some exciting news, she wished her mom was there. But now, her dad tried to fill that role and listen to Abby's questions, dreams, and problems. She was afraid that she would burden him with too much worry over this situation.

"Well, that's a lot of information you just threw at me. What do I think? Well, first of all, I am concerned about you. If someone is trying to hide something that big, sure they will try anything to keep it quiet. I don't know if it is in your best interest to start looking for that person. Does it mean that much for this story to find out what really happened?"

Abby's faced reflected an aggravated expression. "Dad, it's not just for work. I mean, that's important, too, it's my job, but there is a lot more at stake. You know how close I was to Becca. It was only one summer, but we were like sisters."

Abby's dad smiled. He paused to recount the past. "You were pretty close. I don't think you girls spent one summer night apart. She was such a nice girl and was always happy. It was nice seeing you so close with someone."

"Exactly. Think of what you just said: she was always happy. What reason would she have to commit suicide?"

"You never know what is troubling someone. She went through a lot, and maybe she had more problems than you knew about and couldn't take it. Not that it's any excuse, but it's possible."

"I know, Dad, but I knew Becca. She wouldn't do that, and I think I would have known. Tell me the truth. Besides the initial shock from her death, didn't the news of her suicide surprise you?"

Abby's dad looked down at his hands and smoothed a rough part of the cuticle on his coarse fingers. "We were very shocked. Your mother found it hardest to have to tell you, but we both wondered about it. We never wanted to bother the Rices. How can you ask questions like that to a couple that just lost a little girl? We wondered about some unusual circumstances, though."

"If you thought about this before, why didn't you say something? To me? To the police?"

"Come on, Ab. If the town coroner pronounces a death as suicide, who are we to challenge it? Her uncle was the one that found her. She was home alone. Can you imagine the guilt they felt in not protecting her? It wasn't worth the aggravation of stirring things up."

"Well, finding out if someone intentionally hurt my best friend is worth any aggravation to me, even if it is more than ten years later."

"I didn't mean it like that, Abby. Listen, if you have an instinctive feeling about this, go with it. But as your father, I have an instinct, too, and that is to protect you. Just promise me you will be careful with this, okay?"

She knew that was the bottom line. No matter what lay ahead of her and what information she uncovered, her dad wanted her to be safe. She appreciated that. She walked over to him and gave him a huge hug. His powerful arms wrapped around her and made her feel safe.

"Thanks for listening. Paul knows everything that is going on, too," she informed him.

"How is he, by the way, since Jeremy's funeral?"

Abby didn't even mention the theories she had about Jeremy's death. She didn't want to overload her dad with too much information at once.

"Oh, he's okay, I guess. They were close friends. Paul is strong though," she said.

"Tell Paul I asked about him. Am I ever going to meet him?"

"Sure, I'll drop by with him one of these days. We have been busy with work."

"I know. Well, one of these times he will have to stop over. But anyway, just be careful with everything, okay?" He leaned over and rustled her hair.

"I will, Dad. Thanks."

Abby grabbed her bag and bounded out the front door. She felt good now that she had talked to her dad. She felt even better that she had his approval.

Chapter 24

Bob Franklin walked to the back of the room to retrieve a mass card. The desk was cluttered and the dim desk lamp barely illuminated what was in front of him. He searched through the piles of paper that should have been organized. Bob realized that he had to look for someone new soon. He took for granted what Jeremy did for him and how much help he contributed. Jeremy would have taken this place over one day.

An elderly woman approached his desk. Her wrinkled face showed impatience, and her powder-scented perfume was overwhelming.

"Mr. Franklin, we were waiting for a mass card," she prodded.

Her husband impatiently stood behind her. He nodded his head in acknowledgement.

Bob pushed strands of hair to the side of his head and tried to smooth his flustered appearance.

"I was just getting that for you, Mrs. Davis," he said. He slid the card and envelope out of the folder that he finally located.

"I'm sorry to hear about your helper. Jeremy was his name? So terrible that he had that accident," she said.

"Here you go. Let me just get your address again. Um, yeah, we miss Jeremy terribly. The accident was very sad and unfortunate," Bob responded.

"Well, I hope you can find another helper just as nice. Thank you, Mr. Franklin," she said.

The couple walked back into the viewing room as Bob sat in his chair. The wheels squeaked beneath him as he pushed the chair away and looked into the mirrored hall tree across from him. The thinning hair that he kept combing over was a fruitless attempt to camouflage the fact that he was going bald. He looked at his eyes and moved closer, hoping it was the dim light that was casting shadows underneath them. As his breath fogged the mirror, he realized that what he saw was real. It was ever since Jeremy's accident. He closed his darkened eyes at the thought of that word. It made him cringe more than anyone could imagine.

Chapter 25

Abby and Paul went out for lunch. The day was bright and they both needed to get out of the station. They went to Doreen's, taking a chance that it wouldn't be too crowded. They walked in and grabbed the only remaining table. Doreen immediately came over.

"Hey guys, what can I get ya?" Doreen said, greeting them.

"I'll have the turkey club, no mayo and just water, please," Abby ordered.

"Grilled cheese, fries, and a coke," Paul said.

Abby waited until Doreen walked away. "Oh, that's healthy," she teased.

"Well, excuse me, Miss Health Kick. Sorry that I don't run ten miles everyday."

"It's not ten miles, and I just started back up again." Abby wouldn't consider herself on a health kick, but she was happy that she was sticking to her commitment of building up her running stamina. She was at the point where she looked forward to exercising again, and her narrow path that led from civilization to nature was also a source of peace and meditation. It allowed her mind to unravel with the contours of the path.

"Whatever. That's good, though. I have to start exercising again. Maybe I'll start going with you. There are a few good reasons to do that, you know."

"What's that supposed to mean?" she asked.

"I just mean that you should be careful when you are running in the woods by yourself," he said.

She appreciated his concern, but thought he was insinuating something else.

"Or maybe just run somewhere more populated," he continued.

"You've never even seen where I go; it's really beautiful. But anyway, I wanted to tell you about Kim."

"Kim from the courthouse?"

"Yes. I tried calling the Rices, and it seems that they are out of town. I figure we aren't going to get very far with them anyway. Kim said she could run some background searches for me on Colin. If there is anything there, at least we will know what kind of personality traits we are talking about." Abby knew that she wasn't supposed to do this, but she knew Kim since high school; she told her acquaintance to keep it quiet.

"So you still think it's Colin?"

"I'm not saying it's him, but he is a possibility. Regardless, someone wrote those letters, right?"

"Yeah, I guess you're right," Paul said, as he dug into his lunch that was placed in front of him.

Abby knew he couldn't dispute this fact. They both saw it in writing.

"Maybe you can get in touch with Mr. Franklin?" Abby suggested.

"Yeah, let me see. But we better finish up and get back. You are only on until five today, right?"

"Yes. It's going to be nice to be home earlier than seven p.m. If I hurry, I should be able to get a run in before it gets too dark."

"Just be careful. You know what, I'll try to get out early, too, and maybe I can go with you."

"I'll be fine, but if you want to, you're welcome to come…if you can keep up with me."

Paul rolled his eyes and threw his napkin on the table. "If I'm not there by five-thirty, just call me later on when you get back, okay?"

Abby wasn't as excited about having a running partner as much as she was about someone being concerned about her.

* * * *

It wasn't even five when Abby headed out the door. She made it home in record time and shrugged out of her dress pants and sweater and into her faded pants and hooded sweatshirt. The outfit was from college and worn to the point where some might use it for a dust rag, but the comfort level was far too great to discard this garment that she had loved for many years. It wasn't dusk yet, but the day was settling. She would make it a quick run.

As she headed to the back of her house, she paid special attention to the trees that lined the yard. The branches bent in just a perfect manner as to form an archway above the entrance to the woods. Abby never noticed it before, but found it interesting tonight. Usually when she reached the end of the wooded part of the path, she turned back the same way. If it was too dark by the time she would hit the other side of the woods, she would just have to go the long way. She made that run several times as well. When she wasn't crunched for time, it was actually nice going home through the residential area. She enjoyed cooling down and studying the different homes on her way back. People would be bustling around in their living rooms and kitchens. She played a game and tried to figure out what people were doing. Judging by some of the wafting aromas from the homes, she usually passed them during dinner.

The gravel and dirt crunched under her sneakers as she picked up her pace. The mud had mostly dried as the weekly snowfalls of the past winter subsided.

She felt her shoe slacken, and realized her lace was undone. She crouched down to tie it when she heard the sound. Besides her own labored breathing, she heard something in the distance. The soft crunching sound that sounded so familiar during her run was echoed in the distance. It grew closer and Abby stayed still. Her conversation with Paul earlier had her on edge as well as a bit more leery during this run. Then she thought maybe it was Paul. He said he may meet her. Maybe he just missed her at the apartment.

She brought her gloved hands to her face. "Paul!" she yelled. No response. She tried again, but her only answer was the sound of running shoes disturbing the path, closer now. Every second she hesitated made the woods grow darker, and now she figured she better keep running.

She wasn't sure why she was so upset that she heard another runner. There weren't many people that used this path since it started from the back of her house, but it wouldn't be the first time that she encountered another runner or a couple taking a leisurely walk. As she continued running, she could have sworn that the sound was getting closer. She started to sprint and pushed the limits of her heart and lungs. Her legs burned and her chest felt like it was going to explode. She didn't want to take a chance to find out who was sharing this path with her. She saw the clearing that led to the street in the distance. She pushed away some low-lying branches as her feet burned from pounding so hard. She could hear amidst all of this that her fellow runner was definitely not far behind. Abby dared not stop now or turn around. As she reached the street and saw the faint glow emanating from the street lights that were just starting to turn on, she didn't stop and make her leisurely observations of the surrounding town. Her feet slapped against the pavement and her lungs were now on fire. The sweat poured from her temples and the blood pumped profusely through her body. She readied the key in her pocket, and when she reached her apartment, it seemed to take forever to steady her hand and place it in the door.

Once inside, Abby locked the door and fastened the chain. She panicked as she felt like she couldn't catch her breath. After pacing around with her hands on her hips, she bent over and leaned on her knees to calm her breathing.

Abby sat in her bedroom window and watched the trees, waiting for them to reveal someone else leaving the dark woods. She figured whoever was behind her didn't follow her through the town and must have gone back through the path. She looked at the beckoning trees that now framed black emptiness only to see nothing. Her hand shook as she twisted off the white plastic cap from her water bottle. There was no one.

Abby started to feel silly. It could have been anyone on that wooded path, even an animal for that matter. Her mind may just have been playing tricks on her. If she yelled, why did she think someone would necessarily yell back? Maybe they were being just as cautious as she was. Or it could have been Paul and he just didn't hear her. She dialed the number that had become very familiar.

After a few rings, he picked up.

"Hey, did you go running today?" she said, not even giving him a chance to talk first.

"Sorry, the *Seinfeld* re-runs got the best of me. I'm not as dedicated to this exercise thing as you are, I guess. Maybe next time," he said. "You must have gone. Wow, you must have been running pretty hard."

"Why would you say that?" she asked.

"Because you sound like a freight train, you are breathing so hard."

"Well anyway, I have to take a shower. I'm soaked. I will talk to you later," she said and hung up the phone.

It rang two seconds later, and she knew she would have to explain her panicked voice to Paul.

"Let me call you back in a few minutes, I promise."

Abby hung up the phone and looked outside one more time. She sincerely wished Paul had said he went running, but knew all along that it wasn't him.

She checked her locks one more time and headed for the shower. The phone rang several times while she stood under the running water. The hot water felt soothing as it permeated her hair and gushed over her face. As she breathed in the hot mist deeply to clear her senses, she experienced the sharp pain that ran across her chest. She wasn't sure if this was the result of pushing the limits of breathing capacity or just the constriction felt as a result of fear.

Chapter 26

"What do you mean you're not going in today?" Paul asked. He was annoyed that Abby didn't call him back. Every flash on the answering machine was from him. He was concerned about her. Abby's latest encounter in the woods really had him rethinking the situation.

"I have sick days to use, don't I?"

"I know, but I thought work would be good to get your mind off of things, plus we were doing so well on the series."

"There's some stuff I have to get done today." Abby knew what she had to do for some time now. Whether she thought the information was going to fall into her lap or she feared what she may discover, the task to be completed was evident. Her long silences demonstrated her eagerness to end the conversation.

"All right, just call later. Be careful." Paul had been ending many of his conversations with this phrase lately.

* * * *

It had been years since Abby had actually sat down and immersed herself in books. The library was in a beautiful building that most resembled a church. She neither had the time nor need to spend countless hours in this place as she used to during her days at school.

She walked into the lobby and let the door gently close behind her. The enormous ceilings made it impossible to make the air warm in the building. The smell of old books and a slight damp chill made Abby feel oddly comforted. She looked around the large room and held on to her bag slung over her shoulder. Large domes of light hung at the end of their posts that jutted from the ceiling. The empty space looked organized with the perfectly lined up books bordering the scratched wooden tables. Light oak chairs were pushed neatly underneath.

"Can I help you?" the woman behind the desk asked.

"I think I'm okay, but I haven't been here for years. The newspapers on microfiche, are they still downstairs?" Abby asked, pointing to the metal railings on the far wall.

"They are indeed. If you need any help, come see me, hon. It is a light staff during the day. No one is down there today, but I'm available if you need me."

Abby walked over to the staircase. The single bulb at the top of each landing was encased in a metal cage, its dim rays barely lighting the stairwell. Abby gripped the cold metal as she made her way to the basement. The two machines were still in the far corner of the room, and the dusty cases containing the microfiche were on shelves on the opposing side. Two long tables separated the room.

Abby threw her stuff on the faux wood surface and pulled the small notebook out of her bag. She flipped through a few pages and made her way over to the dark aisles that contained years of newspapers. She grabbed the reel from the wall labeled "August 1990, *Watertown Chronicle.*" She placed the film on the spindle and turned the machine on. The low hissing and clicking sound immediately brought back memories of her research in school. As the motor warmed up, it produced a slight burning smell that overpowered the musty basement odor. The noise from this ancient machine was the only thing echoing in this basement. Abby could not hear anything from upstairs and was sure the librarian wouldn't hear her even if she needed help.

Her pulse resounded in her ears as she approached the Obituary section. There wasn't a picture, but the name in bold print still upset Abby. She read the header over and over again; the short date span that showed Becca's abbreviated life was the most saddening. She zoomed in and skimmed through the all too familiar text. Half way down the column, it noted that father, Colin, Railville, PA and her uncle, Jonathan, Watertown, NY, survived her. She didn't know how long Colin resided there and if he still did, but it was her only lead right now. She scanned through two more days of newspapers, searching for some information on Becca's death, but not surprisingly, there wasn't any. She wound the microfiche and placed them back in the box.

After gathering her things, she took two steps at a time as she headed back to the first floor. The basement was not the most inviting of all atmospheres.

The last step was to cross-reference and try to get an address. She sat down in front of one of the two public computers and logged onto the internet.

"Internet access is limited to forty-five minutes," a voice said from behind the desk.

Abby looked around and saw only a bearded man with a heavy overcoat sleeping at one of the tables, propped up by a book. Abby shook her head and kept searching.

"Again, if I could be of any help…" The librarian trailed off.

The woman would not be able to offer the help Abby needed; she had no idea. Abby wasn't sure if she, herself, did either.

* * * *

As soon as she got back to her apartment, she placed everything in front of her on her small kitchen table: the copy of the obituary and the list of names. She dialed Paul's number at work.

"How are you feeling?" he asked.

"Fine, why?" She had forgotten that her reason for calling off was a supposed sudden illness. Once she remembered, she played along. "Oh, I'm much better now. Hey listen, I looked up the obituary in an old newspaper and noticed that Colin used to live in Railville."

"That's about four hours from here. Pennsylvania, isn't it?"

"Yeah, but who knows if he lives there now. I figure it's worth a shot. I have a list of names to check on."

"Abby, do you really think you'll track him down? There's probably several Parsons to contact."

She knew this would prompt such a response from him. "Never mind. I just wanted to get your point of view on this about where I should start. I'll let you go," she said, cutting him short. She wasn't looking for his approval, just his help and a little support.

"Hold on, hold on. Let me guess, you came up with ten names you'd like to contact in that region?" Paul asked.

"Nine, but how did you know?"

"I did a little digging of my own. I referenced the obituary, too, and started looking things up. I didn't make any phone calls yet."

Abby sat back in her chair. Paul was on the same wavelength and could read her mind. She was relieved that he didn't think she was wasting her time. Abby was happy that he cared enough about her and what she thought to help her out without being asked.

"Thanks, Paul, I really appreciate it. Why don't we go over this tonight after you get out of work? Can you stop by?"

"I will. See you later."

Abby felt good about this. She had a plan and it had to happen fast. She called a few of the names on the list but to no avail. She figured she would try one more crucial call that wasn't on the list.

"Hi, Theresa. Abby." She didn't expect a warm response, so she continued. "I know you just got in from out of town, but I just need to ask you something."

The sigh on the other end proved her theory.

"What exactly do you need?" The words were spoken slowly as if Abby couldn't understand.

"I know you're not going to agree with this, but I am trying to look for Colin. All I need from you is exactly the last time you heard from him and where he was living," she said. She left this last statement hanging, almost a question.

"Oh, Abby, enough already. You are beginning to sound like a broken record. First of all, your chances of locating Becca's dad are slim. Secondly, whatever you find out and unsettle will only cause heartache for my husband and the family," she retorted.

Abby wondered to herself who the family was that she referred to. "I understand how you feel and I am not asking you to get involved. I won't mention your name; I'll say I'm from the station."

"No, no. I'm sorry I can't help you. Frankly, I don't know where he is and I don't care. If you let this go, maybe you will be lucky enough not to find him. For everyone's sake, just let it go. None of this is going to bring Becca back."

The words stung even though Abby knew they were true. She knew she was not going to get anywhere with this. Abby wanted to inquire about the journals to see if there was anything jotted down that could help her, but she dared not ask.

"Well, thanks for your time. If you change your mind, can you call me? Let me give you my number again," Abby said.

"Go ahead," Theresa said.

Abby knew she had no intention of writing it down and that she was only humoring her. The realization set in that this was probably the last time she would hear anything from the Rices.

After she hung up, Abby looked at the list and called a few more of the names. An elderly woman picked up on the other end.

"Oh, hi. My name is Abby. I am looking for a Colin Parsons. Is he in?" she asked. She was ready to cross the name off of the list and hang up just like all the rest.

"No, I'm sorry. He doesn't reside here any longer," she said in a quiet voice.

Any longer. Abby sat straight up in her chair and gripped her pen. She didn't rehearse in her mind what she would say if someone mentioned something about the existence of Colin Parsons. Abby didn't want to sound flustered. She took a deep breath and let her reporting skills go to work.

"My name is Abby Greene. I, uh, used to be friends with his daughter, ma'am, Becca. I just need some information. Do you know how I can reach him?" she asked.

There was silence.

"My God, Abby. I heard so much about you from the letters," she said with a quivering voice.

"I'm sorry, I'm confused. I don't think we ever met."

"We didn't, dear, but Becca wrote to me about you in her letters. I'm Becca's grandmother."

Abby dropped the pen to the table. It rolled off the edge and underneath the cabinet. Becca never mentioned her grandmother on her father's side. Abby didn't even know she existed.

Chapter 27

The clock was glowing from her nightstand. She sat up, panicking for a second until she realized what happened. She had been waiting for Paul to get out of work and last she remembered, she rested on her bed for a second, planning out the following day. She must have dozed off. The room was filled with faint moonlight. She didn't leave a single lamp on in the other rooms. Her hallway was a black abyss despite the small, dim nightlight in one of the outlets.

She stumbled into the living room to check her machine. The machine beeped and Paul's voice echoed in the room from three different messages. She must have been dead asleep not to hear them. Paul wasn't going to have a chance to stop over, but he could meet her for a quick cup of coffee if she met him right after at the donut shop.

"Damn it," she said into the still darkened room. She had ten minutes to catch Paul. She needed to race over to the donut shop. She kicked her shoes out from underneath the bed and grabbed her keys and purse.

Abby paused outside her apartment door and listened. She wasn't sure what she was listening for, but she was satisfied that it was safe to run out to her car. She had to catch Paul; her mind was teeming with information about her last two days.

She pulled into the parking lot just in time to see Paul going back to his car. She leaned out her window. When she did, Abby noticed her reflection in the side view mirror. Paul would definitely have to believe her excuse that she fell asleep. She tried to comb some of her hair back into place with her fingers.

Paul peeked in the car.

"Sorry. I fell asleep. I know you said you couldn't stay out late, but I need to talk to you. Can we just talk for a few minutes?" she asked.

"I guess so. But I wanted to go in early tomorrow," he said with a yawn.

As they walked into the donut shop, the fluorescent lights were blinding. This was a far cry from Doreen's relaxing atmosphere, but the strong coffee smelled good and even the remains of the day nestled in the wire baskets on the shelves looked appealing.

As they faced the glass counter, waiting for their order, Abby asked Paul, "Speaking of tomorrow, it's my day off, and I was wondering if you can switch your schedule and get the day off, too."

Chapter 28

"So tell me again about this run. Did you see who it was? I could kick myself for not going. Maybe I would have run into him on the other side of the path," Paul said.

Abby chronicled what happened in the woods the other day. She was so excited about locating Colin that she pushed that to the side; she was too busy to be frightened.

They had about an hour left of their trip until they reached Railville. She was glad she convinced Paul to go. Actually, it was Paul that had to do the convincing. There was no apparent reason why he should be missing a day of work. With his masterful art of persuasion, he expressed to Dave his interest in the small town's tourism and a recent suspicious drowning that had occurred. He needed to do research and already set up an interview with the community's mayor. Abby wasn't sure how much truth to any of his story there was, but Dave bought it.

"I don't know. It was odd. It could have been someone running a normal route, but it gave me an eerie feeling. Regardless, I need to focus my attention on Colin," she said.

"Well I am worried. I told you about being cautious when you run alone. You should probably avoid that area, anyway."

Abby was glad that he repeatedly showed concern for her. She picked up her directions and noted the next exit sign.

"Our off-ramp should be coming up," Abby said.

She looked out the window and thought about what could happen and how she would feel. The lonely turnpike was dull and unexciting. She was sick of the monotonous scenery, interrupted by passing tractor trailers that skimmed their car too closely.

As they exited the ramp, she thought about what she was about to encounter. If she had the chance to talk to Colin, of course he would contest the fact that he had anything to do with his daughter's murder. If it was just Colin's mother, she would do the same. Abby was so surprised that she was able to get in touch with someone that she didn't have much time to think about the full picture. She hoped this wasn't a waste.

As they slowed for the approaching stop sign, Abby reached in the back for her purse. She fixed her make up in the mirror.

"You look very nice today," Paul said.

"Thanks. For a change, right?" she asked. She did look a little more pulled-together than usual. Her black dress pants and pin-striped blouse were things she recently bought. She wore low heels and brought a matching purse. For a change, Abby felt confident about herself and not frumpy standing next to Paul.

She checked her watch; they were thirty minutes ahead of schedule. It was good that they arrived early so they could get a feel for the environment and scope things out.

Paul drove through the town until they got to the bottom of a steep gradient.

Abby studied some of the buildings as they drove through the small city. The narrow street was littered with shops and boutiques. The stores were all connected, each adorned with an ornate and inviting window front.

"If we have a chance, I would love to stop in some of these places. Aren't they adorable?" she asked. The downtown area wasn't big but consisted of more antique shops that she had ever seen. They were scattered on either side, ascending the steep hill. One store, with a beautiful stone façade, was decorated with a wrought iron hanger holding a carved, wooden sign. The etched marker gently undulated in the wind. Abby liked the feel of this place.

"Yeah, they're just precious," he answered in a sarcastic tone.

They turned onto Stern Street and followed Mrs. Parson's directions up the hill and around a few very windy roads. As they entered an open-gated drive, Abby looked down at her paper to make sure they were going the right way.

As she looked up, they rounded the corner and the house came into view. She touched her hand to the window in disbelief. "Oh my God, you've got to be kidding me!"

Paul slowed down before they reached the house and echoed her same sentiments. "Wow, is that monstrous. What an amazing place."

There was a small gravel parking area to the right side that he pulled into. They saw the curtain in the doorway flutter.

"It's a mansion! She told me where it was but failed to mention to look for something of such magnitude," Abby said, getting out of the car without taking her gaze from the beautiful structure.

The house was constructed of faded red brick, complete with turrets and black wrought iron fencing. The foreboding dwelling was eerie but strikingly beautiful. The cobblestone path led to the front of the house, but a small trail that wound around to the side porch looked like the one most traveled. Before they even had the chance to look for a doorknocker, a grating sound and shuffling behind the door indicated that someone already knew they were there. An elderly gentleman appeared before them.

"Ms. Greene?" he asked.

She thought that Mrs. Parsons said she lived alone, but Abby could have been wrong.

"Yes, hi. I'm Abby. And this is Paul. He works with me…at the station." She knew she sounded like an idiot. She couldn't get the words to come out right. Abby hoped the man didn't notice the tremble in her voice.

Paul gave his usual very calm and cool greeting as they entered the foyer.

The door they entered brought them in through the rear of the house. From where they were standing, Abby could see down the hall and noticed two grand archways on either side. The stateliness of the exterior was continued here and throughout the home.

"My name is Owen, Mrs. Parson's assistant. I help her with the upkeep of the house and run her errands. It is such a large home to organize by one's self. I used to work for the historical society and I always loved this home. It has such history. When she was looking for help, I jumped at the chance," he explained.

Abby felt a little foolish. She thought he was a butler. That would fit well in this setting.

"Follow me into the sitting room," he said halfway down the hall.

Abby looked at Paul. He was too busy taking in the intricate designs in the woodwork surrounding them. He was just as enthralled as she was.

They walked into a large room adorned with beautiful upholstered furniture and several plants that seemed to overflow from jeweled or gold vases in every corner. It contrasted greatly from the shadowy wood of the hall that they just walked through. A small woman rose from the couch.

"And you must be Abby. And your friend?" She motioned to Paul.

"My name is Paul, ma'am. I work at WWNY with Abby," he said.

"Well, it's very nice to meet both of you. Owen, would you mind getting us some drinks?" the woman requested.

The man disappeared through the big archway.

Ab thought the furniture looked too delicate to sit on.

Mrs. Parsons must have sensed her caution. "No, don't worry, please sit. It may be antique, but it's still sturdy. Please, both of you have a seat," she invited.

The petite woman sat back on the couch across from them. Her face showed the signs of age, but her appearance demonstrated that she was a woman growing old graciously. Her silver hair didn't hold the normal curl that a woman her age would usually choose. Instead, it was pushed back off of her face and styled to slightly turn under. Her makeup didn't hide the creases in her skin, but the taupe eye shadow and trace of matching lipstick pleasantly accented her face. Her tan flowing tunic was paired with slim-fitting pants that had chocolate beading on the cuffs and matched her sleeves. Overall, this woman who must have been at least eighty, looked more put together than some people Abby's age. "You're home is breathtaking," Abby said as her eyes made a continuous scan of the room they were seated in. The fireplace had a mantle-to-ceiling mirror above it, framed by carved angels. The woodwork encasing the hearth had similar carvings etched in it. The marble base was slightly cracked, but didn't distract from the majesty of it.

"Oh, dear, thank you. I have to tell you, my family comes from a long line of railroad workers and owners. This mansion was built in the late 1800s and served as home for generations of my family. Now, it's just Owen and me. I'm sure he told you that he helps me out with things around here. I'm not as young as I used to be," Mrs. Parsons said with a smirk. "The borough wanted to buy this place and use it as a historical landmark to give tours. I couldn't part with it, so we struck a deal. I would stay here and allow tours during the spring and summer, then on weekends, by appointment only. You'll notice certain areas marked with a velvet rope. We just avoid those areas altogether for preservation. Anyway, it keeps me busy and I get to remain in this beautiful home. But I know you didn't come here to talk about my house, Ms. Greene. You were looking for my son."

Abby was a little uncomfortable with introducing this subject. She didn't want to offend this polite woman, but what she had to ask could come across as nothing but insulting. There was no sign of Colin here that she could see, but she was sure there was ample information about him.

Paul helped her out with this one.

"Well, Mrs. Parsons, Abby and I drove in from Watertown today and we were hoping to get a chance to talk to Colin. If not, it would be great if you could help us out with some of our questions."

Owen returned to the room with a tray. Abby could see shimmering reflections in the polished silver as he placed it on the table. The teapot and cups with saucer were porcelain trimmed with the tiniest floral patterns. Abby couldn't remember ever being served tea in such a style. Mrs. Parsons put a hand up when Owen went to pour.

"I can manage, thanks, Owen," she said.

He took this as a cue to leave the room.

"So, what can I help you with?" she asked.

Abby knew this was coming. She rehearsed it in her mind over and over, even doing a practice interview with Paul on the way to Railville. After taking a deep breath, she went into her explanation of what happened lately. Of course, she stayed away from the fact that they considered her son as a possible murder suspect of her only granddaughter. Abby used the same angle that they used on the Rices: the background information on the station and Abby and Paul's career, the opportunity to do this series on suicide, and, of course, how Abby thought it would be an interesting perspective to get the father's point of view concerning his daughter's death.

Paul chimed in, "Mrs. Parsons, we are trying to cover this delicate subject from all sides. We think it is important to educate not only other young people, but to inform adults as well. If other parents could share their side of the story, we think it may help others."

They both waited for some sort of response from this petite woman that sat across from them, stirring the cubes of sugar in her tea.

"Abby, Paul, I need to explain something to you." Mrs. Parsons didn't take her eyes from her spoon that slowly stirred the warm liquid in the cup.

Abby and Paul used the pause that followed to pick up their cups and help themselves to the strong Earl Grey. Abby let the steam meet her nostrils as she held her cup close to her mouth. She watched Paul maneuver the dainty porcelain with his large hands. She would have to tease him about that later.

"My son, Colin, married Jean when he was young. They were together for a few years before they had Becca. I cannot tell you how blissful he was when that little girl was born. His life was going so well, and his choices that originally seemed so premature fit perfectly into his life." She held a smile on her face and her eyes gazed towards the floor in recollection. With a heavy sigh, she continued, "But then, something happened. Colin started having some problems. He would get very anxious and nervous, which he demonstrated often. I was concerned because there was mental illness that afflicted our side of the family in past generations. I begged him to go for help, but he said he could handle it. I felt sorry for him, but it angered me at the same time. He started getting short with the girls, and that's when I tried to step in. The only problem was he tried to turn it around and make me look like the meddling mother. They stopped coming over for visits, and Jean resented the fact that I was intruding in her husband's life. I stayed away as I watched my son's demise. He lost his job and struggled with finances. My proud son and daughter-in-law wouldn't take *charity*, as they called it. He would disappear for days, only to have Jean calling here looking for him. I didn't house him during his stints of disappearance, but she insisted that I knew. What was I to do?"

Abby was in shock. She never heard any of this from Becca. She didn't even know that the elder Mrs. Parsons was alive.

Paul just sat engrossed in the story. There were no notepads, tape recorders, or cameras, just Paul and Abby giving this woman their attention.

"Then one day, it happened. Becca was still young when Jean called me, crying. Colin had left for good this time. He didn't come here and he didn't go back home. I knew that he was upset by how his life had turned upside down but I was ashamed that he abandoned his family and didn't try to help himself. He ended up moving away and trying to make a new start for himself. He attempted to get his life together. He contacted me several times and told me he was okay. He wanted to get back on track and get back to his family. There was nothing more I could do. The envelope containing money that I sent to Jean was stamped *Return to Sender*. And then, I'm sure I don't have to tell you about poor Jean," she said, tilting her head in sad reminiscence.

"You mean dying of cancer?" Abby confirmed.

"Yes. I never had anything against my daughter-in-law; she just believed that somehow I made her son change for the worse. I thought the best I could do is leave well enough alone if she wasn't going to listen to me. She did call me shortly before her death to let me know of what was to come."

"But why didn't you take Becca in?" Abby asked.

"My first thought was the little girl. I tried to convince Colin to take her in. He said that he didn't feel right walking back into Becca's life, trying to act like everything was okay when he wasn't sure if he was. I offered to look after her, but I found out that Jean's brother and wife were going to be her guardians. I only met them a few times, but from what I understood, they were good people. Becca moved in, and that's when I started receiving letters from her. Becca wanted to come to live with me and she also wanted to be reunited with her father. I tried so very much to convince Colin to attempt to be a father again."

Abby was able to tell that this revelation of her past pained her greatly. With every word that took them deeper into this woeful story, she could see the agony on Mrs. Parson's face. She wrinkled her nose and patted her eyes a few times, but never let the tears flow.

Abby wasn't sure what to make of this conversation thus far. She wasn't certain this was a mother trying to paint a picture of the poor, suffering father that lost his wife and daughter and if any of this was the truth. By the skeptical look on Paul's face and his crossed arms, she knew he felt the same.

After several sips of tea, Mrs. Parsons continued. "You can imagine the heartache we felt when we found out that Becca committed suicide. There were all of the what ifs. What if I talked to the Rices and encouraged Becca to come live with me? What if her father stepped up sooner? Colin really did care about her. Before her death, he would call the Rices to check to make sure Becca had enough to be provided for. They cast him away, since the only picture they had was the one Jonathan's sister painted for them. You can imagine how they felt about me. The death of my granddaughter wounded my son greatly. I don't think he ever forgave himself."

Abby placed her cup gently back to the table. The conversation was leaning towards her next question. She had to ask it.

"Mrs. Parsons, how does your son deal with it now?" she asked, almost afraid to hear the answer.

The woman sat back in her chair and placed both palms on her lap. This time, it was Mrs. Parsons that sighed. "He doesn't, Abby. I not only outlived my granddaughter and daughter-in-law, I outlived my son, as well. They say it was a heart attack that was attributed to high blood pressure. I think it was a broken heart."

Abby was stunned. In all of her rehearsing, she didn't consider this response. Her preparation and direction meant nothing now. She could tell by Paul's fidgeting that he was taken off guard, too. Abby composed herself. The porcelain handle pushed against her knuckle as she clutched the teacup tightly. She swallowed hard and cleared her throat.

"When did Colin die?" she asked.

"About six years ago," Mrs. Parsons replied.

Abby picked up her cup and finished the lukewarm liquid. Her face felt hot, and her heart raced. She didn't even know how to go on with the rest of the conversation. Abby looked at Mrs. Parsons and saw her hand quivering as she placed her cup back on the table. It was then that she realized that her own emotions were not the only ones at stake. If what she said was true, this woman was suffering over the loss of three people very dear to her.

"Mrs. Parsons, I don't even know what to say. I am so sorry about all of this. I didn't know," she said, stumbling through the words.

"Abby, if I wasn't ready to talk about it, I wouldn't have welcomed you into my home. I have a feeling that you didn't travel more than four hours just to talk to me about warning signs of teen suicide. There is something more, am I right?" she asked.

It must have been the urgency in her voice on the phone or Abby's constant shifting in her chair that caused Mrs. Parson to question the purpose of their visit. This dignified woman was smart and couldn't be fooled. There was no need to hold back the real reason they came here in the first place. Paul helped Abby with this decision.

"If you don't mind me saying, Abby, Mrs. Parsons is right. There is something else."

He looked at Abby with his soulful eyes waiting for her approval. She nodded in agreement and waited for him to pick up where she left off.

Paul continued, "We are working on suicide awareness and prevention and want to pass this information on to the public. But there is more to it than that. We have a few suspicions about Becca's death. If it wasn't suicide, we are afraid that someone may be trying to hide what actually happened. Without getting into too many details, there are many strange circumstances surrounding the story."

Mrs. Parsons snickered in response to his interlude. "Well, I would like to tell both of you that I know what you are getting at. Don't you think that I reviewed every detail leading up to the day my granddaughter died? Don't you think I thought about every possibility? I did. I also stopped blaming myself. You cannot blame yourself," she said, turning to Abby. "But, as for my son, he made a few mistakes in life and, towards the end, he was not extremely stable. I can tell you that he loved his wife and daughter but he was afraid. He was terrified that he would continue to fail and that was why he decided to not bring Becca back into his everyday life."

Abby expected this from her. It was her son she was talking about. Mrs. Parson must have read her mind.

"I know what you are thinking. You believe that I may be covering for him. Maybe he is alive this very day and is even somewhere hiding in this house," she said. She moved to the archway, her hand cutting through the air, fingertips leading their eyes to the grand staircase.

She walked across the room behind Abby's chair and paused in front of her. She positioned her hands on her hips and pressed her palm against her head. "I'm sorry. It's just that I want you to know that I loved my son very much. But if I ever thought he hurt my granddaughter in anyway, nonetheless killed her, I would be the first one to turn him in. My son is dead, Abby. And I swear on his grave that he would be the last person to ever lay a hand on Becca."

Paul stood and tried to smooth things over. "We didn't mean to come here and upset you. We are trying to find out the truth. We need to look at all possibilities. We couldn't rule anything out. Abby and I are not pointing fingers at anyone and our concern is as deep as yours in this matter. Like I said, we are trying to look at all angles, and your son was one of the paths we needed to investigate. We needed someone to tell us otherwise, and I think you demonstrated that quite well," he placated. "I think we should not take up anymore of your time."

Mrs. Parsons smoothed a non-existent wrinkle in her slacks. She lowered her voice to a whisper and spoke without looking at the two of them. "I understand your point and I want you to know that I do appreciate your concern. Just please believe me when I tell you that you are looking in the wrong place for your answers." Abby didn't know if this meant she knew where else they should be searching or that she just knew Colin was the wrong place. Regardless, now was not the time to ask that question.

She rose as well and stood next to Paul as Owen returned to the room. They waited for Becca's grandmother to make the next move. She returned to her high backed chair. The slight movement in her body and low sob showed that the resurgence of emotion was starting to take its toll on her. Abby realized that it was now time to leave.

"Please, we are sorry. I thank you for your time, and we will keep you posted with new developments. Thank you again," she said.

Owen stepped aside as they both walked to the foyer.

"Wait, please, for one moment. There is something I want to give to you," Mrs. Parsons said.

She motioned for Owen to come over by her and she whispered into his ear. He nodded without saying a word and then disappeared upstairs. Mrs. Parsons made herself scarce and returned the tray into the kitchen. The two waited patiently in the darkened foyer.

"I don't know where to turn next," Abby confided to Paul while trying to hold back tears. The statement came out as a high-pitched squeak and Paul sensed her sadness and concern. He pushed a tendril of hair away from her face and tucked it behind her ear. She smiled and tried to hold back from crying.

"Relax," he whispered. "Think of it this way: it's just another piece of the puzzle and a step closer to where we are going."

She wished she knew where that was.

Footsteps on the landing ended the brief moment of consoling. They both waited for Owen to reach them. He walked directly into the living room and handed a small photo box to Mrs. Parsons who had just come back in from clearing the tea service.

"Thank you, Owen," she said. She dusted the faded upholstered container and stared at it for a few seconds. She approached Abby and handed her the small box. "I will want these back, but I think it will help if you read through them. They are the letters that Becca sent me. I cherish them," she said.

Abby could tell from her eyes that it pained her to part with her treasure.

"Oh, thank you so much. Why don't I make copies and return the originals to you. I feel badly keeping them out of your possession, even for a few days," she said, tapping on the lid of the box.

"No, just be careful. You need to feel the letters, not just read them. You'll be fine. Return them when you are finished. I trust you," the older lady said.

Abby knew she wouldn't take no for an answer. She placed the box underneath her arm and held out her hand out to Mrs. Parsons. "Thank you again. We really appreciate everything," she said.

The woman's hand was thin and papery and slipped easily out of Abby's. Paul demonstrated his thanks, and they walked with Owen to the door. Mrs. Parsons stood in the entry way as they walked to the car. Abby watched as the huge door slowly closed and the light that glowed behind the stained glass panes was extinguished.

Nothing was said as they got into the car. Abby clutched the letters and ran her fingers over the fraying material and small rusted hinges. She wanted so badly to open and examine the contents but was also so afraid to see what was inside.

"Are you going to go through them now?" Paul asked.

Abby wanted to but figured that fumbling in the car might ruin the fragile paper that sat in the box on her lap. Plus, she didn't fare well when trying to read or study something while in transit. It was probably better to wait. She turned to reach into the back seat and place the box on the floor.

"You know what? I think I'll wait until I get home. It might be difficult reading some of them, anyway. Not that you haven't seen me break down before, but, well, you know…"

Without peeling his eyes from the road, Paul reached over and patted Abby's leg. "It's going to be okay, trust me."

Abby placed her hand on top of his and gave a gentle squeeze. Abby needed to hear that after her world was turned upside down today. It was okay for now, at this instant. The heat from the vent warmed her face, and the soulful crooning of James Taylor played in Paul's CD player. His hand felt heavy and warm on her knee, but most of all, made her feel safe.

Chapter 29

Abby had no intentions of going to sleep until she went through every last letter that she now possessed. Her apartment was dark as she walked in, but she couldn't be bothered with her own fear. She had one agenda and swept everything else from her mind.

The box lay in the center of her bed. She sat next to it and raised the worn lid. A scent from inside wafted into her bedroom. It contained years of mustiness and the light aroma of roses. A wide, pink ribbon bound a stack of papers. Abby ran her finger over the satin bond then slowly undid the bow. She picked up one of the folded pieces of paper and straightened it. It was intact but fragile. The palm of her hand supported the fold. She moved to sit in the window and leaned back against the corner of the wall. It had started to rain outside, and Abby could only hear the light tapping against the window. She felt the coldness that crept through the glass. She looked outside and saw nothing but darkness and the small droplets of water that beaded and reflected the soft light from her lamp. With her knees pulled close to her, she looked down at what she was so eager to read, but procrastinating to see.

Dear Gram,

It sure is nice living out here. Uncle Jonathan and Aunt Theresa are pretty nice. They don't talk much, but I think they feel bad about Mom and don't know what to say. That's okay, though. I met a great friend, Abby. She is in my grade and she likes the same things as me. We play every day. She doesn't have any brothers or sisters, either. I think about Mom a lot and I really miss her. I still wish I could talk to my dad. I like it here, but I would rather be with you and him.

Hopefully, I can visit soon. School is almost over but I still have homework. I love you.

    Becca

Abby read and re-read the letter several times. She looked at the paper that was from a stationary set. It was pink with thin, gray lines, and there was a little girl with a big straw hat and sundress, standing next to a little dog illustrated in the bottom right corner. Abby closed her eyes and envisioned Becca propped up on her elbows on her bedroom floor while she scrawled this letter to her grandmother. The part that she kept reading was the reference to herself. Abby rubbed her finger over the fragile paper and held it up to her nose. The scent of roses filled her nostrils. For the next few hours, she laughed and cried. There were many memories that were stirred up and several things uncovered of which she was not aware. She was very grateful to be able to look back into Becca's past as well as her own.

* * * *

She hit the back of her head against the molding when the sound of the phone ringing jolted her awake. The box lay on the floor with the remaining contents spilled out onto the throw rug next to it. Abby leaned over to look at the clock and realized that she must have dozed off after reading each letter at least five times.

It felt like only seconds, but when the fogginess cleared from Abby's head, she looked at the clock and saw it was three-forty-five a.m. *Who would call her now?* she thought. She didn't have a second to ponder this as she reached for the phone, dropping it once before holding it to her ear. She figured it was Paul.

"Hi," she said, trying her best to sound awake.

There was no answer.

"Hello," she said. At this point, she was very much alert, standing at her bedside.

The other line did reveal that someone was still there, through labored, heavy breathing.

The caller finally spoke in nothing more than a whisper. "Abby, this is your last warning."

Her hand trembled as she clutched the phone. "Who is this?" she shouted.

The familiar click and dial tone ended the short conversation.

Abby slammed down the receiver and paced between her bedroom and kitchen. She didn't know what she was going to do at this time of night but she did know that she couldn't go back to sleep. She peered out into the dark numerous times, seeing shadows that only complicated her mind. With every swaying branch or small, scurrying creature, she was sure it was someone approaching her house and would be at her door any second.

She sat in her living room with a pint of Ben and Jerry's, watching reruns of *E.R.*, watching the clock, thinking morning would never come. Abby knew she would feel better once it was light out.

When she finally saw the sun coming up, and daylight slowly started to filter through her shades, she set her clock so she could get at least two hours of sleep. This time, it wasn't a peaceful slumber that she would fall into.

* * * *

Abby checked the mirror in her car before going into work. Even after trying to pile on layer after layer of makeup, she couldn't disguise that fact that she had barely slept. She pulled her hair back tight and overdid it with the lipstick, trying to take attention away from her sunken, sallow eyes. She knew, however, that Paul would see a bigger problem written all over her face.

Paul was talking to Dave when she walked in. He nodded to her and she acknowledged him. She walked into the break room, praying that someone made coffee, even if it usually resembled sludge. She rinsed out a mug and poured the dark chocolate-looking brew into a cup with no sugar and no cream; she didn't want the caffeine diluted.

Abby walked over to her desk and checked to make sure all of the satellite feeds were set up. She glanced at the rough run down for the noon news and saw Paul walking over. She didn't feel like being at work today, let alone explaining the entire phone call drama to Paul.

"Hey, you still look tired from yesterday," he said.

Great, she thought, *does he mean I looked this bad yesterday?*

"I wanted to tell you, Dave said you got a call yesterday while we were gone. You will be very interested to hear who it is," Paul continued.

"Who?" she asked.

"Mrs. Theresa Rice. She called to see how you were doing and said she was sorry she didn't have a chance to talk to you for a while. They were both away."

"I knew that. I didn't think she would be concerned how I was doing."

"She mentioned that she wanted to talk to you. You should probably call her and clue her in as to what is going on. They might be surprised that Colin is dead."

"Thanks, Paul. I'll get back to her."

Paul quizzically looked at Abby and studied her face. "Are you okay?" he asked. "Really, you look like something is wrong, not to mention that you seem very tired."

"That's just it: I'm tired. Sorry if I seem cranky," she apologized.

She turned her back, and this sent Paul away for the time being. She didn't yet want to mention the part about being scared.

The ringing phone startled her.

"Newsroom," she said without looking at the origin of the call.

"So, are you going to tell me what's wrong or am I going to have to pester you all day?" Paul asked.

She looked up from her desk and shook her head at him. Abby knew she would have to engage him in her situation. She was afraid now and didn't know where to turn.

"It's nothing," she said. She wanted Paul to work a little harder for this information.

"I think I know you by now. Did you find something in the letters?"

"I read through the letters last night. That wasn't too bad. It's just what happened later on. The phone woke me up during the night. It was another threat."

She watched and listened as Paul hung up the phone. He walked over to her desk and pulled a chair in front of her, leaning in to grip the desk.

"That's it. I think it's time to get the police involved. What if there are no threats next time?" he asked.

He looked concerned, and Abby appreciated that. She played around with the idea of reopening this investigation with the facts they had, but she felt like they were so close into drawing this person out. She was afraid that involving law enforcement would scare him away or make him retaliate even harder. She ripped the stray edges of her notebook and purposely ignored Paul.

He knew what she was doing. "You already have your mind made up that you are not going to get anyone else involved, right?"

When she didn't answer, he continued, "Well, you need to talk to the Rices; lay all of this information on the line and tell them that you are going to go to the authorities if you don't find something soon. Maybe that will pressure them to give you more information. I'll go with you after work if you want."

"No, that's okay. I'll go myself. For now, we better get this stuff done," she said, pointing to the pile of papers and references on her desk. "Do you want to take a look at some of these?" She had a few articles quoting statistics on teen suicide in different parts of the country. The extreme Northeast wasn't a high profile area where teen suicide was a problem.

Abby tried to submerge herself in working on their project, but it wasn't playing out as planned. She wasn't prepared to see the Rices tonight. She had other plans that were well past due.

* * * *

As the day drew to a close, Abby gathered her things and walked outside. Mrs. Rice agreed to see her tomorrow. She figured she should call before she made her next stop. Rather than going back into the station, she fished in her pocket for some change as she walked towards the pay phone. She really needed to get a cellular phone.

"Hi, Dad. It's me. Are you in the mood for some company?"

"Sure, but you don't have to ask. Did you eat yet?"

"No, I was going to pick up some pizza. I'll be over soon."

"Sounds good. What's the occasion?"

"Nothing in particular. I haven't seen you in a while and I need to talk. That's all."

That was the first time all day that she felt at ease. Spending time with her dad always made her feel better and gave her a sense of security. She needed an unbiased point of view on what was going on and she wanted a break from work.

It was still light out, so it was easy to spot someone standing near her car. A wave of fear swept over her, but she figured it could be Paul. She couldn't yet make out who was standing there, but as she got closer, she knew it wasn't Paul. The person's stature seemed too big for his build. Abby's heart beat faster, but she looked at the ground and continued to walk forward. She knew that whoever it was wouldn't try to bother her in broad daylight. She realized that he hadn't noticed her yet.

The man glanced at his watch and looked around.

Abby stepped back in between two buildings and watched the man. She wished Paul or anyone would come out to the parking lot at this moment, but she felt as if she was alone with this man standing guard by her car.

Suddenly, he walked across the street and got into a hunter green Bonneville.

Once she thought he was gone, she sprinted to her car. She fumbled with the keys, dropping them in her haste.

Abby pulled out of the parking lot and tore down the street. For as fearful as she was of this man, she wanted to know who he was.

When she got to the stop sign, there was a green car similar to the one she just saw. If the person stalled for time and pulled out at the same instant Abby did, it was very possible they would meet at this intersection. Abby looked at the driver as he passed her. The man in the car gave a short wave and put his head down as if he didn't want to be bothered. The minute she saw his profile, she realized who it was: Bob Franklin.

Chapter 30

Abby balanced the steaming pizza with her one hand as she grabbed her bags. She looked around when she got out of her car. Everything had her on edge since the phone call.

Her dad met her at the door.

"Great, I'm hungry," he said, taking the square box from her hands. He stopped and looked at his daughter. "What's wrong? You look upset."

She knew she couldn't hide anything from her father. She gave him a weak smile, which he answered with a frown.

"There is something wrong. Let's go inside before this gets cold. Tell me in the house," he said.

They walked into the kitchen and sat at the small table. Abby wasn't sure if it was the house or being with her dad, but she felt safe. She changed her focus onto selecting which piece was the best one in the pie. She picked up one of the cheesiest slices and dropped it onto her plate.

"Hey, you took the best piece," her dad said and smiled. This was an unending game that they always played over the years: deciding what the best piece of pizza in a pie was. They always decided on the same one.

Without being prompted, she led into her story. "Dad, I've been having a hard time lately…mainly because I just got another call."

"Another call from that wacko? That's easy. We are just going to call the cops. You should have enough connections at work. If not, I'll just call."

"No, no. That's not how I want to do it. See, I'm working on a complicated story here. I have some ideas, some theories, but it won't sound like I am making much sense if I run to the authorities." She failed to mention that someone was lurking near her car just a few hours earlier.

If she disclosed that, she knew her dad would take matters into his own hands. She changed the subject. "But on a lighter note, I was lucky enough to get a hold of some of Becca's old letters that she sent her grandmother."

"How did you manage that? Do I want to know?"

"Actually, it's a long story, but I have them. It's been a trying few weeks. Then, today, between the phone call and the person by my car…" she said, stopping short.

"Person by your car? You failed to mention that," he said, quite alarmed.

"There was someone walking around my car after work today. I just got a little spooked. I think I know who it was. I have to check a few things out, though."

"Just remember, if you feel like you're in trouble, I don't care who won't understand, we are going to call the police," he said, lecturing like a true parent.

"Yeah, yeah, I know. Do you want to watch a movie? I need to laugh," she said, ending the conversation.

He knew exactly what that meant. He walked over to the cabinet beneath the television and held up a copy of *Major League*. It was one of their favorites. She bought it for him a few Christmases ago.

Her dad popped in the movie, and Abby grabbed some snacks. She felt safe tonight and promised herself she would remove herself from all worry and fear. Laughing with her dad for a few hours did the trick.

After the movie, she rummaged through her bag and took out her weathered gray T-shirt and flannel pants. She headed to her old bedroom. Her dad still had her furniture and twin bed just the way it was. It was nice to see. He said it was the guestroom, but she knew he just couldn't bring himself to move his little girl out. This added to her sense of security within these walls.

She remembered that she wanted to call Paul before she went to bed. She wasn't going to, but also didn't want to alarm him if he couldn't get in touch with her, not to mention she wanted to hear his voice.

"Goodnight, Dad. I'm going to bed as soon as I call Paul," she said, turning into her old room.

This time, her dad smiled and wagged his finger at her. "There we go with Paul again. I will meet him soon, right?" He didn't wait for an answer nor did he see Abby roll her eyes.

* * * *

The next morning, she woke up to find her dad already bustling about. She rested in her old bed, her hands propped behind her head, thinking if only she could just lie there all day, all week, secluded from the outside world where all of her problems lay. But that wasn't how it worked; that wasn't what she needed to do. She wasn't a teenager anymore and able to hide from her problems.

With that, she swung her feet over the edge of the bed and rested her hands on the mattress. She looked at the worn, wooden floor, scarcely covered by the old throw rug. The sunlight danced off the smooth wood surface, illuminating small dust particles. She was stalling to begin her day, but the dark, roasted coffee brewing in the kitchen drew her out of her room.

She walked into the kitchen, not seeing her dad. Reflexively, she went to the cabinet above the sink, but found Tupperware and plastic bags instead.

"I moved them to the cabinet on your right," her dad said as he walked in with the newspaper tucked underneath his arm. "Sometimes I get bored, so I do a little rearranging."

Abby opened the door and peered inside for her favorite mug. It was a large, gray cup, which held what seemed like a bottomless amount of coffee. She added her four sugars and even more sweetened creamer to lighten the black liquid. She wasn't concerned about diluting caffeine today; she had slept well. There was a small chip in the mug's handle that was familiar to her. She ran her thumb over the imperfection, like she usually did during conversation with her parents. She knew she would burn her mouth, but she sipped from her mug anyway.

She wasn't planning on going to work today, although she knew the excuses were only going to last for so long. She didn't forget about her goal, though. She knew what had to get done, and that played on her mind, too.

"You're nervous today, aren't you?" her dad asked.

"I'm just thinking about everything I have to do today. I should get ready. But I wanted to thank you again. I'm glad I stayed here."

"Me, too, Abby girl, me, too. Now go get ready," he said, motioning with his cup, the coffee sloshing over the side.

Before she walked out the door, she called Paul one last time. "Hey, it's me. I'm not going in at all today. I told Dave I wasn't sure if I could make it in today anyway. Tell him I will definitely be around tomorrow."

Chapter 31

Abby drove, unsure the entire time if she should be making this first stop. She didn't think it would pose a threat to her, but if for some reason it did, she felt safe. She reached into her bag and touched the small, slender canister that rested in the front pocket. She never had to use it, but the mace was there if she ever needed it.

She pulled up in front of the funeral home and sat for a second to gather her thoughts before she walked to the door. She was interested to see the expression on Bob Franklin's face when he saw her. At least she thought she was. She rapped on the door once and stepped back. She straightened her jacket and tightened the low ponytail. There was no turning back now as she heard footsteps grow closer.

She cleared her throat as he opened the door and extended the first greeting.

"Mr. Franklin, hi. I was wondering if I could talk to you for a minute?" she asked. She studied his face, but his expression was hard to read. It was one of shock mixed with fear.

He didn't answer at first, but when she looked past him into the foyer, he jumped back in embarrassment and beckoned her to come in.

"Can I take that for you?" he asked, motioning to her bag.

She wanted to keep it near just in case. "Oh no, I'm fine, thanks."

He led her into the sitting area. The room, although void of flowers, still had the lingering eerie smell. They sat in two puce, velvet chairs, topped off with brass upholstery buttons.

"I was on my way to visit someone, and I wanted a chance to stop by to talk to you. I hope I'm not keeping you from anything?" she explained as Bob constantly scanned the room.

"No, I don't have any viewings scheduled today or tomorrow, but you never know, right?" he followed with a nervous laugh. It was a poor attempt at funeral director humor. His nervousness carried over in his voice and in his non-stop writhing hands. He cut the small talk and the jolliness dissipated as his tone lowered a few octaves.

"Abby, listen. I know why you are here. Let's cut to the chase. You saw me by your car the other day, didn't you? You are not here to talk about the weather." He stopped and paused, waiting for her as she nodded in agreement. "So, do you want to know what I wanted?"

Abby didn't say a word. All of a sudden, she felt overpowered by him in this conversation. Her assertiveness was left at the door.

"I wanted to talk to you for quite sometime. I think you should let this thing with Becca go. I wanted to warn you before," he said.

This is it, Abby thought. *How could I have been so stupid?* It was Franklin that had been harassing and trying to scare her. She should have asked Paul to come with her today. Franklin probably couldn't believe how easy she was making this for him. She felt hot now, tugged at her collar, and grabbed her purse tighter.

"I don't know you that well, but I know that you are a good person. I'm just trying to warn you to be careful. I don't want anything bad happening to you…like it did to Jeremy," he continued.

She stood up from her chair and stepped back. "You killed Jeremy?" she asked, backing up towards the door.

"Killed him? Abby, I'm still trying to deal with his death. It haunts me everyday. Look, I'm not the bad guy here. Please, sit down."

Abby cautiously sat back on the chair, ready to run out at a moment's notice. She listened intently. "The Rices tried to warn you, and I am going to tell you again: be wary of Becca's dad, Colin. I know you probably heard that he was dead, but you shouldn't be so trusting."

"You mean the fact that he might still be alive? I am aware of that," Abby added.

She continued her press for info about Jeremy.

"What did you mean when you said that something bad happened to Jeremy?"

"That's something I don't know for sure, but let me explain. You started asking questions about Becca, and that ignited a chain reaction. Paul talked to Jeremy and helped to resurface things that he hadn't talked about for years. It really upset Jeremy. I told him not to worry about it and that there was nothing he could do now. I knew he wouldn't let it go. He got a few phone calls here that were extremely troubling, but he never told me who it was. Then…the accident."

"So you don't think it was an accident?"

"It could have been, sure, but it's odd that he starts poking around in this matter again, and all of a sudden, the road that he traveled a million times gets the better of him. It strikes me as odd. You have to understand: I don't just miss him as a worker, I miss him as a friend."

Abby could tell by the look on his face that he was rattled.

"I don't know if Colin is playing a part in all of this, but if he has a dark past, he might be pretty upset that someone is unearthing it. I am trying to help you," he finished.

Abby absent-mindedly played with her silver ring. "How did you find out about Colin?"

"I talked to Becca's uncle, Jonathan. We are close in this town, you know. He thinks it is Colin."

"But why wouldn't anyone go to the police with any of this? It's ludicrous. If you think that's what happened, find him and be done with it." Abby searched Franklin's eyes for answers, but he looked at the floor instead. "Well?" she pressed, waiting for a response.

"It's just that Theresa and Jonathan Rice suffered enough. They don't want to get the police involved at this point. I am just telling you to be careful."

She realized she wasn't going to get any further with him. Her suspicions had ridden back and forth over the past thirty minutes, but she didn't fear Bob Franklin. She knew there was something that he feared; that was what she needed to find out.

"Well, I thank you for your time, and I will probably be calling you soon. Thanks again," she said, shaking his clammy hand. She coiled back and couldn't wait to get to her car.

* * * *

Abby called the newsroom before her next stop. Paul answered. She heard him furiously typing in the background.

"If you are busy, I can call you back," she offered.

"No. Hey, before you stop anywhere else, meet me at work."

"I am supposed to be off sick today."

"I'll meet you in the parking lot, okay? How about ten minutes?"

"I'll be there in ten or fifteen."

She made it there in less. Abby pulled in to the far end of the parking lot and met Paul.

He motioned for her to put the window down and leaned in. "How is everything going?"

"Okay. What's going on?" she asked, irritably.

"I just wanted to tell you that Dave really wants us to start wrapping up our series, maybe doing two more installments. We have to get it finished."

"I know, I know, I'm just busy today," she said, the aggravation coming out in her voice.

"That's not all I wanted. Here," he said, handing her a cardboard box.

She looked at it, trying to figure out what he could possibly give her in this shoebox-size package.

"Open it. It's nothing, really. If you don't want to keep it, you can cancel." He smiled and shrugged his hands into his pockets as she undid the lid. A palm-sized cell phone was inside.

"A cell phone?" she asked. She had been meaning to get one, but never got around to it. She never had the extra money to buy one.

"It's just with all of your running around, I thought it would be better if you had one. But like I said, if you don't want it…"

"Oh no, I love it. Thank you, Paul." She reached over and kissed his cheek. That was one of the most thoughtful things anyone had done for her. Not the fact that it was a gift, but the meaning behind it. He must care about her enough to be that worried about her safety. She got a chill and smiled at the thought that someone was thinking of her to this degree.

Abby explained that she had to get to the Rices and drove away. After a few miles, she pulled to the side of the road. She struggled for a few minutes trying to figure out how to turn the thing on. Paul must have already set everything up in it. He had their work number programmed into the speed dial. She depressed the small button.

"Paul Triver," he answered.

"Hey, it's me."

"Boy, I can see it already: you'll be cursing me when your bill is so high, right?"

"No, I just wanted to call and thank you, again. You don't know how much I appreciate it."

"I am so glad that you do."

Chapter 32

Abby's foot was heavy on the gas and her mind was swimming with several thoughts. Theresa told Abby to call before she came over, but she ignored that request.

The house loomed in the distance. Abby saw two cars in the driveway and breathed a sigh of relief. Her shoes crunched over the gravel driveway as she made her way to the porch. She didn't even have to knock. Theresa was there, waiting.

"Abby. I thought you were going to call before you came over," she said with surprise.

"I'm sorry. I was off work today, so I thought I would just drop by. Is it a bad time?"

"Well, actually—"

Mrs. Rice's sentence was halted by a yell from upstairs. "Who's here?" Jonathan asked.

"It's Abby. I didn't know she was dropping by." Theresa shot Abby a wicked glance, reiterating the fact that she was annoyed with Abby's presence.

"Look, I can come back," Abby said. That wasn't her intention, but she offered it to smooth the tension.

"Come in, come in. We needed to talk to you anyway." Theresa made an exaggerated swing with her arm, letting Abby inside.

"Thank you, I won't be long. I just needed to ask you a few things."

"That's fine, Abby. No really, it's good to see you. We have been so busy lately and it was hard to get in touch with you. Can I get you something to drink?" Jonathan asked as he came down the stairs.

"I'm fine. Really, I just need a few questions answered." Abby didn't hesitate to explain what she was getting at. "You know what's going on. Yes, Paul and I have been working on the series on suicide prevention, but it stirred up a bit more. It is mainly about Becca's death. I know it is a sensitive subject for you, but I have some information that the facts we possess may not be correct. Someone is trying to stop me from finding out the truth. I know it's difficult, but could you please tell me again about the day you found Becca's body?"

Theresa and Jonathan looked at each other.

Theresa was the first one to speak. "Abby, we told you this was a challenging subject for both of us, especially Jonathan. It's been many years, and we still carry the pain. But we are tired. This is only bringing back horrid memories and making it very difficult."

Before Abby could even respond, Jonathan chimed in, "Theresa, it's okay. I can speak for myself. Becca was my niece and I cared for her very much. I know you did, too. We have dealt with all of these issues and have come to terms with ourselves. We know that no matter what we do or say, or how much we beat ourselves up, it's not going to bring her back. Abby, we wish as much as you that there was something we could have done. Imagine my reaction when I thought our little girl was sleeping and I shook her and she didn't wake. The bottle was on the dresser and that was that. The coroner ruled it a suicide. It's a simple explanation to a very complex matter."

Theresa grabbed Jonathan's hand and rubbed it gently. He looked like tears were welling up in his eyes.

Abby didn't really know what to say next, but she knew what she had to accomplish. "I know this is hard, but do you think there is any chance foul play had a role in this? I know Theresa mentioned to me that Colin was not a stable man."

"Yes, I know my wife discussed that with you, and we both talked about this before. Colin knew money existed from his wife's trust, but I can't believe he would do something to hurt his only daughter. And what would he do? Force her to take the pills? It just doesn't add up. I tried to convince Theresa of the same theory," he said.

With that comment, his wife dropped his hand and looked away.

Abby had to get what she came here for. "Jonathan, I realize all of this, but why would someone want to stop me from investigating what happened? Why would I receive threatening phone calls and letters?"

"All I can say about that is it is probably a coincidence. Maybe it's some wacko who knows your background and is trying to give you a little scare. I really don't know what to tell you, Abby, but I don't think you have anything to worry about. Maybe you should talk to a counselor about dealing with all of this."

Abby didn't say anything about guilt or grief. Jonathan was just trying to make her seem like the irrational one who still had issues. She knew she wasn't going to get much further with them.

"Well, thanks for your help. I'll think about what you said. Thanks again for your time, and I am sorry if I bothered you," she said, heading out the door.

"No bother, Abby. We just want you to be okay, too." Jonathan tried to sound compassionate.

"I appreciate that," she said as she left the porch. "I'll call you if I need anything else."

Abby drove away, glancing back as the couple stood on their porch with Jonathan's arms around his wife. It was obvious that they were not going to help her out anymore. They basically told Abby they washed their hands of this. The problem was that Abby couldn't let it stop there. However, she knew she wouldn't be talking to them again anytime soon.

The ride home wasn't long, but it seemed to take forever. Abby was tired and mentally worn out.

As she walked into her apartment, she placed her leather portfolio bag on the table and stared at it for a few seconds. She pulled some of Becca's letters out that she carried around with her and stared at them. Her plan was to return them to Mrs. Parsons soon. Abby felt as if she couldn't read them enough. She examined them over and over and hoped some bit of information would jump out at her. She placed the aging papers in a pile and cried. Her tears turned into long sobs and she was grateful no one was there to witness her breakdown. Everything was taking its toll, and she felt like she didn't have the right answers for anyone, not even herself.

Her self-pity was interrupted by Paul's call.

"What's wrong, Ab?" he asked, alarmed after hearing her quivering voice.

"I don't know, just everything," Abby said. She tried to explain, but knew she wasn't making much sense.

"Wait, how about I'll just come over and see you?" he suggested.

This was exactly what she wanted, but didn't want to ask.

Before long, there was a knock at the door.

"Hey, there. How are you?" he asked.

"I'm all right. Thanks for coming over." She shifted her weight from one foot and lowered her head. Her emotions were taking control again.

Paul walked in and gently shut the door behind him. He placed a bag on the counter and fished in his coat pocket for his keys.

"See, I always come prepared." He held up the bottle of wine that he pulled from the bag and the corkscrew that miraculously appeared from his key chain. "Glasses?" he asked, pointing to the cabinets.

"The one over the stove."

He poured two glasses of the deep burgundy wine and handed her the thin, stemmed glass.

"Thank you, I needed this." She sat back on the couch and pulled her knees in close to her. The wine was dry but had a pleasant aroma with subtle hints of oak.

She broke into her spiel. "I'm sorry about before. I know I sound like such a whiner. Everything just got to me today. This entire situation with Becca has me whirling around. Then there is work. All my life I wanted to be a journalist, but yet I am doing nothing to help myself. I keep putting off what should have been accomplished in a few weeks. I am sure Dave has no respect for me, let alone ever thinking of promoting me from the news desk. I keep involving everyone into my problems and then I complicate their lives. And who knows to what extent? I mean the whole Jeremy thing. Then my dad is harping on me, instructing how I should call the police. And then there is you. I care about you so much, and I know I am going to screw that up, too." Abby stopped. For a few minutes, she had let her emotions unleash, but the last sentence brought her to a halt. She couldn't believe what she just said. Things had progressed nicely between her and Paul. Their friendship had developed into what she thought was something deeper. Now, she was afraid how he would respond to her verbally admitting it.

"What was that?" he asked. He moved closer to her and sat back with his head propped up by his hand on the back of couch.

"Paul, I'm sorry. I didn't mean to say—"

"Abby," he interrupted.

"No, really, I'm sorry. I'm just bringing you down, and you have to deal with this paranoid girl."

"Abby," he said louder.

"You are probably sick of hearing me whine, just like tonight."

This time he didn't say her name. Instead, he leaned in close and moved his hand up to her face. He gently pulled her towards him, tilted his head, and pressed his lips to hers. She couldn't open her eyes. His mouth lingered next to hers. She didn't want it to stop. When he pulled his lips away, he just stared. He ran his hand down her cheek, wiping the tears. For the past few minutes, she ranted and raved and now she was at a loss for words.

He read her mind. "You don't have to say anything. You already said all I needed to hear. I also want you to know the image you portray. You are a determined woman who has high aspirations and goals that I know you will achieve. I see a girl who cares about her friends, even old friends. I also see this beautiful, caring person that makes me smile every time I see her. I am going to help you with this, Abby. I'm happy that I am involved, because if I wasn't, I wouldn't have had the chance to get close to you."

Abby leaned over and kissed him again. They embraced, and she felt safe. She knew that her affection for him had been growing for months, but didn't realize how much. Abby never dreamed that he mirrored these thoughts.

For the remainder of the evening, they talked and laughed together, as they had in the past. But this time, it was different. They were on a new level now. However, there was one thing that she needed to ask him.

"What are you doing tomorrow?" she asked.

"After work, nothing. Why?" he asked.

"Let's have dinner with my dad," she invited. "I think it's time for you to meet him."

They made plans for the next day then went back to discussing what they needed to do next for their story. Abby liked his ideas. If they were going to find out exactly how Becca felt before she died or if there was any fear or animosity towards anyone, there was only one person they could get that from: Becca.

Chapter 33

"Don't you look nice today," Paul said.

Abby shot a glance and frown towards him. She wasn't sure if there was a no dating policy at station. She didn't even know if they were considered dating, but whatever it was, she was content.

"I can't say you look nice?" he asked in response to her glare.

"Thank you," she relented. Abby wasn't used to dressing up this much for work, but today was different. She had on a slim black skirt with matching shoes, just a little higher than she was used to wearing. Her crisp, white blouse and thin silver necklace gave her a confidence level that she normally didn't possess. When she walked into the office, Abby didn't feel like slumping behind the assignment desk this time. Part of her plan was to wrap things up with the project. Then, she could move on to the second part.

Abby walked into the dressing room and checked her hair several times. She had done some narration for the previous stories but not on camera. Dave and Paul both decided that she should conduct one of the interviews. She was happy to add something new to her demo tape.

She walked back into the studio and reviewed her notes about Karen one last time. She didn't want to walk into this blindly.

Abby entered the lobby to find the young girl sitting in the corner of the room. She was checking her compact and fiddling with her hair.

"Hi, I am Abby Greene. You must be Karen?"

"Hi," the petite girl responded and gave Abby a weak smile. She bit the corner of her lip and looked at Abby. "Do I look okay?" she asked.

She had on the typical dress for a high school student these days: baggy khakis and a tiny tee-shirt.

"You look fine. Why don't you come back with me to the studio?" Abby invited, walking down the short hall.

The girl was a sophomore in high school, but she looked so young. Her hair was long and strawberry blonde. Her complexion was fair and dotted with several freckles. She looked so innocent, but mainly, she looked scared to be here. Abby gave her credit for coming out and talking about her experience. She had lost a friend to suicide only a year ago. Karen was hopefully going to answer some of Abby's questions about how she was coping and if she had seen any signs.

After over twenty minutes of an emotional interview, Abby only had a few more questions to follow up with.

"Karen, is there anything you would say now to help your peers be aware of situations like this?"

Karen paused for a minute then said something that Abby knew too well. "I miss her a lot, and I think that there will always be a part of me that will think that I could have done something to prevent it. Now when I look back, there were signs, but that doesn't help her, or me, now. I would just tell kids to listen to their friends and look hard. If they are reaching out for help, give it to them."

Abby just nodded her head. She tried to be a good listener.

"Thanks, Karen. Hopefully your advice and your story could prevent a tragedy such as this in the future."

Abby pulled the lavaliere microphone from her blouse and leaned over to help Karen.

"Was I okay?" she asked.

"You were great. You are a strong person and a good friend, Karen."

By the smile on the young girl's face, she could tell that this saddened teenager needed to hear that. Karen leaned over and gave Abby a hug. She didn't bring up anything about Becca because this was Karen's story, not hers. Abby walked her back out to the lobby.

"Thanks again, Ms. Greene. You are doing a good thing."

Abby smiled and showed Karen to the door.

As she walked back into the office, she hoped that she could convince herself of that, too. Abby went right back to work, helping with the editing. Everyone complimented her on the interview and said it went very well. Abby was pleased.

Her next obstacle would be introducing Paul to her dad tonight.

* * * *

They went directly to her dad's for dinner. She was nervous about Paul meeting him. Her dad was an easygoing guy, and Paul was a great person to bring home to meet. Still, she felt fluttering in her stomach and her heart beat rapidly.

They walked up the steps, and Paul grabbed Abby's hand, giving it a squeeze before her dad came to the door. Paul sensed her nervousness. He whispered in her ear to relax. She was more nervous than he was.

"Well, you must be Paul. I've heard so much about you. Come in," her dad said, welcoming them.

Abby thought that was a cliché greeting, but it worked. Her dad was just as nervous as she was.

All three went inside and proceeded to the kitchen.

"So how did the wrap up of the series go today?" her dad asked as he lifted a huge pot of noodles off of the stove.

Her dad was a great cook all though he rarely used those skills. Abby was pleased to see that he was making one of his best dishes: ziti and meatballs. The sweet sauce was one of her favorites.

The strong smell of garlic bread emulated from the oven as the door creaked open. Abby got up to help him.

"It went well, Mr. Greene, thanks to your daughter. This new reporter stepped up today and did a fabulous interview. We did all of the editing, so it should air in the next day or two."

"That was fast. And please, call me Mike. Is that the last one?" her dad asked.

"One more after that, just a final overview," Paul answered as he helped himself to a big portion of the homemade sauce and steaming noodles.

Abby felt one hundred percent relieved. She was afraid it was going to be awkward starting the conversation. Both Paul and her dad fell easily into talking with each other. She could tell from the way her dad treated Paul that he approved already. Abby caught her dad glancing at her a few times during dinner with a smirk on his face. That was a good thing.

After a great dinner, Abby helped her dad clear the table. He whispered to her that Paul was a nice guy. Abby shushed him, although she was elated to hear that.

"What, I am just saying that he is nice and that I approve."

"Well, I wasn't looking for your approval. I just wanted you to meet him." Even though she wouldn't admit it, Abby knew that an approval was a big reason she brought Paul over here tonight.

Much to her embarrassment, her dad went to pull out old pictures.

"Aw, what a cute kid," Paul said while leafing through page after page. The album crinkled as Paul turned the plastic covered vinyl. "And you are just as cute now," he whispered while Abby's dad went into the kitchen to get coffee for the three of them.

The night wound down, and Abby put all of the photo albums back on the shelf. She told her dad it was going to be a busy day tomorrow and that they should get going.

"Thanks, Mike. Everything was great. It was nice meeting you," Paul said as he shook her dad's hand.

Abby knew her dad was impressed by his strong handshake. The first day she met Paul, she noticed the grip that would squeeze the fingers off of your hand. It gave her dad's a run for his money.

"Take care," her dad said. He gave her a kiss on the cheek. "Goodnight, Abbygirl."

"Goodnight, Dad."

As they walked down the steps, Paul turned to her and said, "*Abbygirl.* I didn't know you had a nickname."

"Mom and Dad always called me that."

"Your dad is a nice guy. I enjoyed tonight," he said.

They reached her apartment, but he stopped before coming in.

"I'm not going to stay. If you plan on getting up early tomorrow to get an early start, you should get some rest. I just want you to know that I do care about you and I want you to be careful. All the times in the past that you were concerned about something or worried, I was concerned, too, even if I didn't show it. You know, that day you were running…"

"You mean the day that I thought I was being chased?"

"Yeah…no, it's nothing…I just wanted you to know that I was upset when you told me," he said, backing out of his speech.

Abby gave him a quizzical look. She wasn't sure what he meant by that or where it was going.

Paul quickly changed the subject and gave her a short kiss. "Listen, I have to go. I will talk to you sometime tomorrow, okay?" He placed his hands on her shoulders.

"I will get in touch. Thanks again for coming tonight," she said.

Abby walked into her apartment and tried to figure out what just happened. She thought they were having a great time, and then all of a sudden, Paul froze. Maybe meeting her father was too much. She couldn't think about it now, but she knew these feelings could surface from becoming too attached. She tried not to dwell on it.

Abby sat in her window. The glass felt cool against her arm as she pulled her feet underneath her trying to contain herself in this, her own private segment of the world.

Two hours passed as she browsed through Becca's letters. She knew she would have to return them tomorrow. Abby just wanted to hold these traces of her friend's existence a little longer.

As she placed them next to the frame containing the picture of her and Becca, she heard snapping twigs outside. With little moonlight, she couldn't observe much. Abby turned her back to the window and placed the pink pages back into their resting place. She ignored the noises outside and instead, walked to the front door to see if it was locked. She checked it three times as if the first wasn't good enough. It was most likely the wind anyway.

She tried to call Paul, but there was no answer. She figured he stopped somewhere after dropping her off, possibly even back at the station. Abby left a message for him and got ready for bed. Tomorrow was a day that she wasn't sure she was prepared for.

Chapter 34

The numbers on the clock glowed back at her that it was five a.m.

With her eyes half opened, Abby walked into the kitchen and turned on the stove. The living room was still dark except for the flickering television. She sank into her couch, aimlessly wandering through the channels. After flipping through old *Scooby Doo* cartoons and several paid programs, she realized there was nothing worth paying attention to. For someone that worked at a television station, she really didn't watch much TV, especially the news.

She threw the remote onto the chair as she walked over to the whistling teapot. The steam billowed out and hissed as she carried it to the counter. She sat there and finished her oatmeal and drank her coffee.

Her mind was working, trying to put her day together and analyze if her plan would work. The atmosphere was so still and quiet. It was too early for anyone to be stirring.

The spoon clinked as she placed it in the sink. The dull light shone over the stove and it still took some time to get accustomed to light. Her clock above the sink read five-twenty a.m.

She stared at the second hand going around and decided that it wasn't too early. She should really get started.

By the time she got on the road, it was six-thirty a.m. There was a fog still lifting that would add some time on to her trip. She was happy that she was up early.

The car behind her hugged the curve and quickly moved in close. This annoyed Abby since the fog could lead to a quick fender bender.

She pulled off at the next rest stop to wait a few minutes.

"Buy a cinnamon bun get a coffee free this morning," chirped the young girl behind the Cinnabon shop as Abby entered the rest area.

Abby was tempted but knew she could do without the sweet roll. "Maybe later," she replied before walking into the institutional-looking restroom. The coffee *did* sound good.

She looked down the long row of stalls. It was as quiet in here as it was in her apartment this morning. The dented, aluminum doors and dull tile added to the coldness in this place. She was surprised that the rest stop wasn't bustling with commuters or passing tourists. She walked into one of the stalls and hung her purse on the hook behind the door. Just as she clicked the lock, she heard a shuffling outside the door.

"Relax," she said to herself. *Why was it odd that someone else was in a public bathroom?*

The shuffling stopped and Abby noticed a pair of black shoes and pants underneath the door to her stall. There was no reason for someone to be waiting and this caused Abby to panic. She pressed her hand against the cool, steel door, not knowing if she should fling it open or wait.

The grating sound and thump of the main door made her jump back.

"Yeah, I've been on that diet before. It doesn't work. You couldn't have cinnamon buns on that," clamored a boisterous woman.

"I hear ya, and while you're away, you don't want to count calories, right?" another other woman responded.

Abby heard water running. She pushed the door open and bounded out of the stall.

"Hey, watch it, miss," one of the bejeweled, overweight women said as she made an exaggerated step back.

Abby looked up and down the row and didn't see any signs of the black shoes and pants combination. Without waiting to find out where that person was, she ran out the door.

She pulled her phone out of her purse and searched through the numbers that she had saved. "Hi, Mrs. Parsons? I hope you don't mind that I am going to be a little early," Abby said. She juggled her purse and keys and scanned the parking lot as she got into her car.

"That's fine, dear. Is everything okay?" the woman asked. She must have heard the nervousness in her voice.

"Yes," Abby lied.

Chapter 35

It seemed like it took forever, but Abby finally pulled up in front of the daunting structure. She tucked the box underneath her arm and ran to the front door. Owen greeted her.

"Nice to see you again, Ms. Greene," he said, holding the box of letters as she shrugged out of her coat.

Mrs. Parson looked as polished as ever, her rose perfume filling the air.

"Mrs. Parson, I told you a lot last time I was here, but there are some things that I left out. There are some details you should know," Abby said.

Mrs. Parson sat, intently listening to Abby's well-rehearsed stories. She knew it was all or nothing at this point and she couldn't hold back. After taking a breath, she waited for a reply. Mrs. Parsons turned to Owen instead.

"Owen, can you get our coats?" she requested.

Abby was confused. "Do you need me to drive somewhere?" she asked.

"No need. We are just going for a walk."

They made the way down the steps and around to the back of the house. The sun seemed to be sprayed on every shrub and flower, as it bounced its light through the remaining morning dew. Abby didn't realize before, but the landscaping was just as beautiful as the home itself, even in these early spring months. The sculpted hedges that surrounded the property were perfectly maintained. The view was spectacular. They followed a stone path that passed a small pond. A few large goldfish were swimming around, and Abby stopped for a minute to watch them as their golden scales shimmered through the crystal water.

They continued down a small road that was bigger than a bike path, but didn't seem large enough for a full size car. They were met with an oxidized iron gate. Mrs. Parson's frail hand lifted the clasp on the closed entrance.

They kept walking until they reached a slight hill. They followed this until Abby noticed a slanted roof jutting out of the side of the knoll. Mrs. Parsons fished in her pocket for something as they stood in front of this stone structure. It was now that Abby first realized that Owen was not walking with them.

The elderly woman produced a round hoop that held several keys. She studied them for a second and fit a slender skeleton key into the black gate on the front of the structure. The metal scraped against the stone floor as beautiful color danced around inside. This was created from the exquisite stained glass window that was almost the entire length of the back wall. Up until this point, Mrs. Parson's did not utter a single word.

"Many families that date back generations will keep private cemeteries on the property. We opted for something a little grander," she explained.

Abby looked around the small mausoleum. Despite the beauty of the artwork that graced the stained glass and the polished stone, the place was one of death. It sent shivers down her spine.

Mrs. Parsons started talking about different family members buried here and stopped in front of one stone marker at the end of the row.

"And this, Abby, is my son, Colin Parsons. If you had any doubt whether he was alive or dead, hopefully this is proof. I told you before, but I think you need to see it. Look at the dates, Abby. Listen to my stories. My son did not kill my granddaughter."

They stood there in silence, staring at Colin's name. Abby touched the cold stone and traced her fingers over the engraved letters.

"I don't know exactly what happened to Becca, but I know where you need to look. I think you may find what you are looking for there."

The silence that enveloped them was broken by the sound of water dripping somewhere in the mausoleum. Abby stepped out into the daylight and felt relief from the dank, cold structure. She waited as Mrs. Parsons secured the door again.

"Mrs. Parsons, if you don't mind me asking, why wasn't Becca buried here?"

"I ask myself that question many times over, and you may be able to get that answered as well. You need to talk to Jonathan and Theresa Rice. I am sure they have more answers to your questions than I do."

"So they didn't want her buried here?"

"They didn't want many things. Talk to them, Abby."

They approached the house, but Abby didn't plan on going back in. She thanked Mrs. Parsons for everything, especially for the letters, then she hugged the thin woman.

"I know you miss Becca as greatly as I do. Just promise you will take care and keep in touch?" the older woman whispered.

"I will. I promise. Goodbye, Mrs. Parsons," Abby said. She knew what she needed to do. It was not necessary to further their conversation.

As she got back into her car and looked for her phone to call Paul, she noticed something on the seat beside her. It was the box containing Becca's letters. She looked up at the porch to see Mrs. Parson waving to her. She disappeared into the house. Abby knew how much those letters meant to the elderly woman yet she entrusted them to Abby. Tears streamed down her face as she made her way back to Watertown, dialing her phone. She tried to hold back sniffles as Paul picked up.

"I just wanted you to know that I am on my way back. I have to go to the Rices. Mrs. Parsons insisted that I talk to them. I will explain everything later. I wanted to let you know where I was going in case you were looking for me."

"Do you want me to go with you?" Paul asked.

"No, I need to do this myself. I will call you later."

"Take care, Abbygirl. Be careful."

Abby laughed and said goodbye to Paul. Her phone beeped after ending the call. She rummaged for her charger when she realized that she didn't bring it with her. The battery was low, so she shut it off and placed it back in the glove compartment. She wanted to save what she had left in case she needed it later. She stretched her hands against the steering wheel and settled in for the ride back. First stop: the Rices.

Chapter 36

Abby turned onto the road that had become very familiar. The monstrous trees reached over the road, forming an arch. Dusk had begun to grace the sky, painting it with subtle pink and blue hues. Once she passed through this entrance to the Rices' house, the trees shaded her from the splendid colors. Their cover made it seem darker than it really was. Abby never realized how barren this stretch of roadway was. She hit the gas and accelerated her journey. Dirt and rocks kicked up, plinking against the windshield.

Once the dust cleared, she rounded the corner and saw that there were no lights on in the home. They probably heard her noisy arrival and thought it to be nosy tourists. She figured it wouldn't hurt to knock on the door. Abby parked her car as close as possible to the porch. She rummaged in her glove compartment and found a small flashlight. After hitting the base a few times, she managed to produce a beam of light. She tucked it into her pocket and stepped out of the car.

Before Abby made her way to the house, she heard it. There was nothing. The light wind barely made a sound. Abby realized that is why people flocked to this region. It was calm and serene. This way of life removed from the chaos and noise of the city was something to be appreciated. Abby realized that she took all of this for granted. For a few seconds, Abby felt like she was alone in the world. As peaceful as it may have seemed, it also made her uneasy.

Abby looked around and didn't see signs of anyone. She stepped to the door and tried it anyway. The echo of her rapping disturbed the previous serene moment. She was aggravated that no one was able to allow her entry into the house. This was not working into her plans. She would have to try the back door. It was possible someone was home but didn't hear her. When her attempts proved to be futile, Abby found herself on the front porch once again. The home was empty as daylight crept away and darkness of twilight started to take its place.

She figured she would come back in an hour or two to see if anyone was home then. Abby needed to complete this tonight.

She ducked into the car and heard only the sound of her leather jacket as she sat in the seat. That's when she noticed the slanted cellar door on the side of the home. All of her possibilities were not yet exhausted. The front door was secured, as well as the back door. Besides scaling the house and trying a window, the Bilco door was her best shot.

The wind picked up and rattled a gaudy wind chime on the side porch. She knew that she had no right entering the house without the Rices' permission. But on the other hand, it's not like they didn't know her. They may not like that she was intruding, but she doubted they would do anything about it.

Abby's mind was set. She rehearsed the plan in her head, hinging on the fact that the handle that she grasped would give when she yanked on it. She planned on entering the basement through the doors and would then shut them behind her. She would then head upstairs to unlock the front door. That way, if she heard a car coming, she could just run upstairs and stand in the foyer, saying that the door was unlocked and she thought she would let herself in. She would say she thought maybe one of them was home and didn't hear her. The best part of this plan was that she wouldn't have to explain why she needed Becca's journals. She would already have them.

Abby tugged at the doors that wouldn't budge. They didn't feel like they were locked, just stuck. They probably hadn't been opened in years. She placed both hands on the rusted handles and pulled with great force. She fell backward onto the ground, but sitting in front of her were the two doors stretched open, exposing the gaping hole into the basement. Abby wiped the copper flakes from her hands and tried to peer into the cellar. For as happy as she was that she now had the access she needed, a part of her wouldn't be too upset if she was getting back into her Honda right now and driving away. She grabbed her flashlight and stood in front of the doors.

"Come on, Ab, just get your foot in the door," she said out loud. She laughed at the unintentional pun. As she planted her shoe solidly on the first wooden step, Abby crouched down, trying to see inside. Her beam of light did not reveal much, except for the dust particles that danced in the light. She tapped her foot as she felt for each wooden step. Finally, she made her way to the dirt cellar floor.

"Now where is the light?" she wondered, again conversing with herself. She felt along the wall and scanned with her light for a switch. She found one, but it did nothing more than cast a forty-watt glow over the expansive area. The dimness, though, was better than complete darkness.

The large room also had two hallways that branched off in two directions. She wasn't sure where each empty looking passage led, but she knew she would have to have a plan of attack in place soon.

Before venturing farther, she remembered the door. The easy exit beckoned her to run back up the steps and head home. That was the easy thing to do. She paused for a second then grasped the handle, folding the doors over her head. The metal clamored as the doors fell into place.

She made her way back through the room, shining the white beam over old cartons of decorations, bottles of wine, and an ancient sewing machine. The boxes holding Becca's journals were not in sight. She knew Theresa brought them down, but she didn't know where to begin looking in this massive area. Abby knew she had to do something soon. She could explain her way out of being in the foyer, but explaining why she was lurking around the basement would be a little more difficult. She didn't try to kid herself that she wasn't afraid. She had no idea how she stayed down here as long as she did, but she knew her bravery wouldn't last much longer.

Her eyes grew accustomed to the dimness surrounding her, but the blackness of the two halls in front of her would propel her into complete darkness. She marched down the right hall at a quick pace, as if moving faster would make it any easier. As she discovered the lighting for this room, she noticed the box immediately.

A scratching noise from behind made her jump. She spun around quickly, splaying the light. There was nothing that she could see.

She hurried and dug into the box. She was thrilled to find the journals so quickly. Abby reached in and grabbed a few of the notebooks. Whatever she could comfortably fit in her jacket was all she would be taking home. She didn't want to get caught with these, of all things, if the Rices happened to come home.

Abby directed the beam of light over the familiar writing. She thumbed through some of the pages. There were more good memories to be uncovered, but Abby knew she had no time to reminisce now. The last few pages of the second journal dealt with Becca's mom, dad, and grandmother. Abby was about to close it shut and tuck it in her coat when the last entry made her stop.

"You have got to be kidding," she whispered. She leaned against the wall as she followed the prose with her flashlight. She knew her time was valuable, but not as important as what she uncovered. She figured the Rices never read through all of these, otherwise, the pages probably wouldn't exist right now. If she thought her heart raced when she first entered this dank cellar, it was now ready to explode. She tried very hard to digest what was in front of her. She continued reading.

It's been several months since I moved in with Uncle Jonathan and Aunt Theresa. At first I thought that I had to get used to living here. But now I know that I am just unhappy. I miss Mom, and it's been such a while since I've seen Dad. All my aunt and uncle talk about is that money Mom left for me. They keep saying Dad might try to come and take it and that I should be careful. It really makes me sad that they talk about him like that. I really don't like this place and I wish I could leave.

Abby welled up while reading this. *Could this be it? All that time, Becca was depressed and she never talked about it?* These past few months, Abby had worried about murder suspects and thinking that someone was after her. *Could it be that Becca really did kill herself?*

Abby took the next journal in the box and tucked it under her coat. She placed the box back where it was and decided to leave. She could look at what she clutched close to her body later. It was growing late and she didn't feel like confronting the Rices at all. Now she did feel foolish.

Abby turned the light off and went back down the hall. She focused the beam of light towards the steps and made her way over. Just as she reached the first step, she felt something brush against the back of her head. She froze, waiting for someone or something to make a sound. There was nothing. She slowly turned around and only caught a glimpse of a dark figure.

A hand clamped over her mouth and pulled her back. She tried to scream, but the powerful grasp prevented her from breathing, let alone making a sound.

She dropped her flashlight and kicked her feet wildly. Her breathing became difficult and her struggle all but vanished. The fabric that covered the gloved hand was rough as it pushed against her face. She felt as if her nose would fracture from the pressure at any second. The pain was excruciating and the burning sensation extreme. The powerful smell nauseated her. She tried to lunge forward one last time, but that attempt was the last thing she recalled.

Chapter 37

Paul headed home after work. He hadn't heard from Abby for a few hours and hoped that everything went well at the Rices.

As he walked into his apartment, the first thing he noticed was the flashing red light on the nearby table. The automated voice that responded when he hit the button told him he had six messages. He was sure they were from Abby. He turned to throw his keys and wallet on the table while he listened to the first message.

"Hi, Paul. It's Bob Franklin. If you could call me as soon as possible, we need to talk."

He was surprised to hear from Mr. Franklin, and even more shocked to hear that the remaining messages were all from him.

He was playing the last message to catch the phone number one more time when there was a knock at his door. He looked out and saw a nervous Bob Franklin standing and waiting. Paul opened the door.

"Hey, Bob. What's going on?" he asked. There was no time for small talk. He wanted him to get to the point.

"Can I come in? I've needed to talk to you for some time, now, and I know this is going to sound crazy… Well, listen, can I just come in first?"

His quick speech and worried look had Paul curious. They walked into the living room and Paul put on the rest of the lights. Bob's chest was heaving as he sat down and stared at Paul.

"Have you talked to Abby today?" was the first thing he said.

"Earlier this morning. Why? Is she okay?" At the mention of Abby's name, Paul started to get concerned.

"I don't know anything about her right now, Paul, but you have to hear me out. There is a lot that I have to explain. This is probably going to implicate me down the road, but I don't care at this point. This has to do with Becca. You know how the Rices took her in years ago because she had no other family, right?"

"Yeah, except for her grandmother."

"Right, but her grandmother was declared too frail to care for her granddaughter," Bob said.

"Too frail? I met the woman, and she seems fine now almost twelve years later," Paul exclaimed.

"I know, I know. Jonathan had a lot of connections, and he persuaded the courts that it would be in their best interest to award custody to him and his wife, Theresa. They weren't stupid. They knew Becca had an ample trust fund set aside to help with her expenses. After she moved in, they also found out something else: Becca had the power to delegate what monies were to be spent on her. Sure, there was the set dollar figure for her caregivers to provide for food and housing, but the rest she decided to keep for college. Quite frankly, it was enough to let her live comfortably when she was eighteen. We are talking over a million dollars here," Bob explained.

"So, okay, where is this going?" Paul asked "Paul, Becca didn't commit suicide. Jonathan and Theresa paid someone to come into the house and have her murdered. They didn't want to get their hands dirty in the whole thing. The person they hired suffocated Becca. They set it up like she overdosed. After her death, her guardians would inherit her trust funds."

Paul had a sickened feeling in his stomach. He wasn't sure he wanted to hear the rest, but he knew there was much more to this story. He would hold his extraneous questions until later.

"How could you possibly cover up something like that? I mean, the coroner would notice that the cause of death was something other than a drug overdose, right?" he asked.

Mr. Franklin sat there looking at his hands. When he looked at Paul, his eyes looked like two glass orbs teeming with water. "Do you know what Theresa's maiden name is?" he asked between sobs.

"No. What are you talking about? What does that have to do with anything?"

"Theresa is my sister. They called me right after Becca was murdered. I can't explain it now, but at the time, I felt like I had to protect my sister. I was the only funeral director in town at the time and I also served as the coroner."

"Oh my God," Paul said.

Bob continued, in tears. "I raced to the house before the police even got there. When I arrived, it was only Jonathan and Theresa there. They acted the part right from the beginning. They were crying and carrying on about their poor Becca. Two police officers arrived shortly after and came over to me. I told them it was a suspected suicide. We walked upstairs to find her limp body on the bed. The police saw the bottles next to her and they looked to me for answers. So, I pronounce her dead; cause of death: suicide. My God, Paul, it was an awful thing that I did. I know I am just as guilty as my sister, but I was only thinking about Theresa at the time, protecting her. Plus, there was money in it for me. The Rices acted like they were grieving over their niece that just committed suicide. The town coroner confirmed that it was indeed a suicide. There was nothing to investigate."

Paul sat there with his head in his hands, not able to digest all that he just heard. Without even picking up his head, he spoke to Bob. "I've heard enough for now. We will deal with that later. What's going to happen to Abby?"

"That's what I need you to do. We have to find her. I got a call from Theresa earlier, and she sounded bizarre. I don't know what they are up to, but I can't live with myself if something else happens to someone. All of these years, I lived with this guilt, and then after Jeremy…"

"Holy Christ, Bob. Don't tell me they killed him, too?" Paul yelled.

Bob continued to blubber like a crying child. "I don't know, I don't know. But if they thought he knew too much… I just don't think it was an accident," he admitted. "That's what made me have second thoughts. He was like a son to me. I could never live with myself if his life was wasted because of all of this, too." He wiped his nose on his sleeve and rubbed his eyes.

Paul was already pulling on his coat. He picked up the phone before he left.

"Hi, Mike, it's Paul. I just wanted to let you know that Abby and I are going over to the Rice's house. If you don't hear from us in a few hours, call the police," he said.

"What? The police? What are you talking about? Where's Abby?" Abby's dad asked.

"She's fine. I just have some things to discuss with them and I am afraid it may get heated. Just trust me, and I will try to call you later. Hopefully, there won't be any need for the police."

Paul got Abby's dad to agree. He mainly wanted someone to know where he was in case something happened. He wasn't sure Bob Franklin was that person to trust.

As he walked towards the door, Franklin followed him.

"Come on, Paul. I would call this time if something happened," he assured.

"Right now, I really don't know what you would do and I can't deal with that. I am going myself. Don't try to disappear; I know the story now. There is no more hiding," Paul said as he waited for Franklin to step outside.

"Good luck, Paul. I just hope we are in time," Franklin called to Paul, who was running for his car.

"You better hope we are in time."

The tires squealed as Paul raced away from the curb.

Chapter 38

Abby woke up and felt something cold against her cheek. Once she gained her composure, she realized her hands were bound behind her back. It took her a few foggy moments to realize what had happened. She remembered making it to the cellar steps then struggling with the unidentified stranger. Her lungs hurt when she tried to breathe and her mouth felt raw. She tried to piece everything together. Her main focus was breaking loose from her restraints and trying to make her way out of this cellar, assuming that was where she still was.

She was afraid, but the adrenalin pumping through her veins gave her the strength to pursue a way to break free from the ropes. She didn't have much time to think about her fear. Abby heard murmuring close by and strained to listen, but couldn't make out the words. She decided not to make any noise since it would be better if whoever was near by thought she was still out.

Abby rose to her feet and struggled with the rope that bound her hands. Amazingly, she was able to wriggle free from her restraint.

There was no light filtering in from anywhere. She moved her outstretched arms in front of her as she walked. She encountered a door with no handle and then the smooth, damp wall.

As she slid her hands across the cold stone, she stepped on something. She bent down and felt the substance surrounding her feet. Abby picked up what felt like a small piece of rock and touched its smooth surface and rough edges. It felt like coal. She figured by the perimeter of the room she was enclosed in, she was in an old coal bin. "I told you I would find her, and that's it. My job is done. That's it for my end of the bargain. You figure out the rest," she heard a man in another room say, raising his voice.

"Shhh," another softer voice whispered. They either knew Abby was awake or didn't want to wake her.

With her ear to the door, she tried to make out the voices.

"Fine, we will take it from here. You realize that your silence is part of this deal. It would be in your best interest to stay quiet," the same voice said.

"Listen, lady, I know what I have to do, don't worry," the man responded.

Abby heard footsteps and then a door open and close. She knew that she had to make a break for it. By catching her attacker off guard, she may be able to make it to that door. She stepped onto the coal and it made a cracking sound under her feet. The door flew open.

"Hello, Abby, nice to see you," Theresa said. "Were you looking for something? Maybe we could help you? Could you step out here?"

Jonathan stood next to Theresa, wielding a gun.

Helpless without a weapon, Abby decided not to fight back. She felt sickened by the sight of these two people, and fear easily crept back into her, along with disgust.

They forced her down the hall, back to the dimly lit area that she visited before. She felt the hard tip of the gun shoved in her back as she was pushed towards a chair near the far wall. The chair creaked as she was forced to sit down. "Why? Why are you doing this?" she asked. She was surprised to find her voice sounded strong.

"Oh, Abby my dear, why?" Theresa said in a mocking tone. "We gave you several warnings. You should have stopped playing Nancy Drew a long time ago and this would have been avoided. But no, you kept prying and prying and getting closer and closer. For years, Abby, we were able to let this go. Then, Little Miss Social Issue has to do a story on teen suicide." She held her hands up in a mocking fashion and rolled her eyes. "We never expected you to talk to Jeremy," she continued as she tightened ropes around Abby's hands again.

"Jeremy? What does he have to do with this? Did you kill him, too?" Abby asked.

"We didn't kill him, Abby, he just had a bad, bad accident," Jonathan answered. His smile was eerily cold.

Abby couldn't believe that Becca's own flesh and blood were involved in such horrific acts. Abby struggled against the newly bound ropes.

"Relax, dear. You're not going anywhere," Jonathan said. "Try to understand: I never wanted to take my niece in. Theresa and I had too much going for us. But then we realized the money that was involved if we took care of her. Of course, then we found out the inheritance was all hers unless she met a tragic end first. And what a sad situation when poor Becca killed herself. But, money is money, and it had to go to someone."

The smug look on his face made Abby want to vomit. She started crying instead.

"You people are twisted. And if you think you are going to kill me, there will be someone right after me to finish this story. I'm not the only one that knows," Abby threatened, tears streaming down her face.

"But you see, Abby, it's the complete end to your series. Maybe Paul could even finish it. How ironic, the girl that is telling the sad story of her friend's death and other suicides commits the tragic act herself. It's so sad," Theresa said in the same singsong voice.

Theresa's knees crackled as she stooped down next to Abby and hissed into her ear. "The emotions and memories that were resurrected brought on a great depression. She went to the home of her dead friend's uncle, symbolically killing herself. Wow, what a tragic tale." She pretended to dab at her eyes. "I could see the movie now," she mocked.

A cold chill passed over Abby. Besides digesting the information that Becca's own aunt and uncle killed their niece, they were planning on doing the same to her. She tried to stay as calm as possible. "You won't get away with this. There are experts that will investigate this and realize it wasn't a suicide. You'll both be in prison for the rest of your lives or worse." Abby tried to use some psychology to divert the pair.

"Nice try, Ab," Jonathan said. "But when you have a brother-in-law who is a mortician and the county coroner, it makes the cause of death that's filed very credible. It worked so far."

"Brother-in-law? You mean Colin?" Abby asked, confused.

"Colin? Colin is dead. I mean Theresa's brother, Bob Franklin. I'm surprised you didn't figure that one out."

Abby was shaking but tried to stay calm. "No, but I do have Becca's journals. She started suspecting that the two of you were plotting to take her money. She was afraid for her safety. It's all in writing and I have copies."

Jonathan paced back and forth as he scratched the back of his head.

"She's lying, Jonathan. Why do you think she was coming here in the first place? To get the journals. Anything written about us is still in this house and it will be destroyed. We covered our tracks." Theresa walked away from her husband and leaned against Abby again. Her sarcasm continued. "And when the police come to question us, we will be so upset. All of the memories will bring back the sorrowful time when we lost our little Becca."

A loud noise echoed from upstairs. A crash rang out.

"What was that?" Theresa barked. "Jonathan, you better go and check it out. I'll stay here."

Abby could tell by the look on her face that this rattled Theresa. They obviously had a plan, and whatever made the noise was not part of it. Jonathan exited out a door that must have led to the kitchen. This gave Abby a chance to try to talk to Theresa.

"You know they are going to find everything out. I talked to your brother and he is willing to help me," she lied.

"Abby, you are not going to be around to receive help with anything," she said.

In light of the threatening words, Abby tried to remain calm. "So, let me ask you: was it you following me all of those times? And the phone calls, too?"

"Jonathan and I had nothing to do with it ourselves. Do you think we would risk getting caught? We had someone hired to do that. Like I said, we gave you ample warning to let this go. It's unfortunate that it had to come to this."

Abby worked at sliding her hands free again, but this time, the twine was tied tightly. The rope burned as it dug into her wrists. Her skin felt sticky as they slid against one another. She knew she was bleeding.

Theresa kept her eyes focused on Abby as she backed up towards the door. She poked her head into the frame yelling for her husband. "Jonathan, is everything okay?"

Abby watched her as she leaned into the archway. She had on blue tailored pants and a gray and blue striped oxford. By looking at this polished yuppie, Abby would never have thought she was the mastermind behind this web of murder and deception. Abby knew that there was more behind her façade, and that was what she was afraid of. She knew that if she was to try to get out of this room, now was the time. Abby's hands were tied tightly, but they weren't tied to the chair. She strained her arms back as far as she could and pushed with all of her strength. After she lifted her arms around the back of the chair, she sat back down and waited for Theresa to step back into the doorway.

"We are going to have to go up there to find out what's going on," Theresa decided as she turned back into the room.

Abby waited until she moved closer to chair. She knew she had to make this work on the first attempt. Before Theresa could realize that Abby's hands were no longer behind the back of the chair, Abby stood and rammed her knee into her side. As Theresa doubled over in pain, Abby kicked her with all of her might in the knee. It knocked her to the floor.

"You little bitch," Theresa hissed, gripping her side and moaning in pain.

Abby ran past her, knowing she only had a few seconds until Jonathan discovered what had happened. She jumped over Theresa's arm and fell into the doorframe as she was pulled back. Theresa grabbed her ankle and yanked her to the floor. Abby hit her face on the lower step and felt a new stream of blood cascading over her chin. She kicked at the hand that grappled to bring her down and landed her heel against the side of Theresa's head. Abby looked up the steps expecting to see Jonathan and continued when she didn't. She fumbled with the door at the top of the steps and pushed it open with her shoulder.

The cellar door led her into the foyer. The house was dark . Abby made her way into the kitchen and struggled with one of the knives to loosen her restraint.

After cutting her hands several times, she cut the rope and ran into the hall. There, standing at the bottom of the steps, was Jonathan, gun in hand. Her triumph now turned again to fear and despair.

"Abby, going somewhere so soon? You are a feisty little thing, aren't you? I don't think this suicide thing is going to work out. It's just going to be easier to have you considered a missing person. They'll never find your body, and it might just work out better after all. If I didn't get in trouble because of Becca, I'm definitely not going to get in trouble because of you."

Jonathan approached her with the gun and backed her into the kitchen. Her hands were still streaming with blood and her jaw was numb. Her palm slipped when she reached for the countertop behind her. She turned her head and winced. Gun shots resonated through the room. Abby was still standing. Jonathan fell forward, and the gun slid across the floor.

"Abby, grab the gun," someone screamed. It was Paul.

Jonathan was still alive, but Paul wrestled him to the floor.

Abby grabbed the gun and held it, pointing at Jonathan. She never held a gun before, let alone fired one.

Now, Jonathan had Paul pinned to the ground with his fingers clamped around his neck.

"Leave him alone!" Abby screamed.

Jonathan turned and looked at Abby for a split second. His eyes raged and bared the window to the soul of an evil human being.

"Why? You won't shoot me." He laughed.

Tears filled up in Abby's eyes, and her hands were shaking as she tried to keep the gun as far away from herself as possible. She steadied the weapon the best she could and aimed for Jonathan's shoulder. The recoil from the gun made her jump back, and the resonating sound was deafening. Jonathan rolled on the floor, blood oozing from beneath his hand clutching the wound. Abby dropped the gun and slumped to the floor against the cabinet. The room started to tilt as she looked at her crimson hands.

"Abby, move!" she heard Paul scream.

She looked up and saw Jonathan coming towards her, his shirt soaked with blood. She stood up and reached behind her for the same knife that broke her free. She held it in front of her as Jonathan plowed towards her. He wasn't giving up. He screamed something at her, and she plunged the knife deep inside his stomach. The feeling of that blade searing through flesh made Abby sick. She felt like she was going to vomit and pushed Jonathan away. He fell to the floor, both hands on the knife. His eyes were wide and his mouth was open in a twisted grimace. The room started spinning and Abby slid down the cabinets back to the floor. She felt cold and tingly as she watched the pool of blood grow larger in front of her. Paul was trying to talk to Abby. He crouched down and pulled her close to his chest. He smoothed her hair and tried to calm her.

Abby sobbed and tried to tell Paul about Becca. "Paul, they killed Becca, they killed Becca," was all she could say.

"I know the whole story. We are going to get the police involved this time. We will tell them everything. Where is Theresa?"

"She's downstairs, but I think she is hurt," she said. Abby heard sirens approaching the house. "Did you call the cops already?"

"No, but I guarantee that your dad and Bob Franklin did. I told both of them to stay out of it until I needed them, but I am sure they called the police as soon as I left."

Abby sat on the tile and didn't move. She looked at Jonathan lying on the floor. She couldn't believe she killed someone, but she saved herself and she saved Paul. If she only knew twelve years ago what she knew now, maybe she could have saved Becca. She cried as she looked at the blood-stained floor that surrounded Jonathan.

She spoke out to his dead body. "How could you? How could you?" she stammered.

She pulled herself up from the floor and walked over to the door. The cruisers were pulling up just as she peered out the window. They ran up the steps, guns wielded, bursting through the door.

Abby put up her hands as they pointed the gun at her. "I'm okay, I'm okay. I am Abby. There is one person dead in the kitchen and another one hurt downstairs. My friend, Paul, is still in the kitchen."

The officers barged through the cellar door and went to retrieve Theresa. Paul let them pass as he made his way over to Abby. She wanted to hug him but was too weak. He grabbed her instead.

"It's going to be okay, you know that, right? It's all over," he comforted.

"I know, but it's all in the journals and then Jeremy, did you know that—"

Paul cut her off. "I know everything, Abby. Bob Franklin told me what happened. I am just as stunned as you are. My main concern was you."

Paul looked at her face. He tried to wipe away some of the blood and soot. This made Abby cry even more.

"So if Bob didn't talk to you, you wouldn't have known to look for me and then…" Abby said, with the reality of what happened sinking in.

"But I did find out, and you are okay. I told you I wouldn't let anything bad happen to you."

He pushed the hair away from her face and pressed his lips against hers. His kiss felt good and there was no doubting where their relationship was. The pain in her jaw dissipated for a few seconds as he drew her pain away from her.

Paul whispered into her ear, "I am so glad that you are okay. I don't know what I would do if something happened to you," he said, his voice quivering.

This was the nicest thing Abby heard in her life. The next best thing followed seconds later.

"Abby, are you all right?" her dad yelled, running towards her.

She broke away from Paul's embrace and replaced it with her father's.

"Dad, it's terrible. Do you know what they did to Becca and to Jeremy? It's so awful," she cried. The reality and truth of what actually happened started to hit her.

"It's a hard thing to understand how people work like that. I'm just happy that you are okay."

Abby saw the police talking to Bob Franklin outside.

"What's going to happen to him?" she asked.

"Well, technically, he is an accomplice to murder by not revealing the true nature of Becca's death, among a slew of other offenses. But he promised to testify against his sister and Jonathan," her dad informed her.

"Well, now just his sister," she corrected.

Her dad looked at the crumpled body on the floor, then continued, "They are also going to investigate Jeremy's death. What Franklin did was wrong, but believe it or not, he is living with such guilt, and now with Jeremy, he knows that he is going to have to pay for what he did…or what he didn't do."

Abby looked at everything going on around her. An officer threw a white sheet over Jonathan's body. All of this reminded her of when they found Becca. "I should have done more to help her," she stammered.

"You uncovered all of this. You risked your life to find out the truth. That is one of the biggest sacrifices a friend could make," Paul said, rejoining them.

Chapter 39

The next day, Abby hoped she was awakening from a nightmare, but she knew that she had just lived through it. Her raw wrists served as a grim reminder. She winced as she touched her face. She didn't even want to look in the mirror. A wave of relief did pass over her when she realized that this was now coming to an end. She still had a lot of questions and grief to deal with, but for now, she knew she was safe and she had found what she was looking for. It didn't make it any easier to handle, but it put her mind at rest just knowing. She was sure Becca would have felt the same way. She was able to bring the right people to justice and erase the tarnish of suicide from Becca's name. Just then, she remembered what she wanted to do last night and made her way over to the phone.

"Hi, Owen, it's Abby Greene. May I speak to Mrs. Parsons?"

There was silence for a moment.

"Ms. Greene, I have terrible news. Mrs. Parsons passed away last night. She has been sick for some time now. I've been here to take care of her. She did receive a call from your friend Paul earlier in the day. He explained the entire story about Becca."

Abby was stunned. She didn't even know Mrs. Parsons was sick. "Did she say anything, Owen?"

"She told me to tell you thank you."

"Thank you, Owen." Abby knew then that it was fate that she met Mrs. Parsons. Whether it was Becca working through her grandmother or not, she was sure someone made it a point to get the right information into her hands.

Abby walked over to the window and looked outside. It was a beautiful day. The sun danced on the ledge, illuminating the picture of her and Becca. She picked up the frame and looked at her friend. "Thanks, Becca."

Abby placed the small wooden picture frame back on the windowsill.

Chapter 40

Abby straightened her suit and fixed the lavaliere mic on her jacket.

"Do I look okay?" she asked, clearing her throat. Her bruises were covered as best as possible, but she thought her face still looked swollen. Her blouse disguised her butchered wrists.

"You look great," Paul assured her. He moved out of the way so the cameraman could adjust his angle. "Just remember, don't be nervous. You'll be fine."

"That's easy for you to say. Talk about jumping into the fire."

She knew several stations were taking this feed, and she got numerous calls about her story. Abby didn't expect Dave to want *her* to cover it.

"This is your story, Abby," he had said.

She didn't know if this helped ease her nerves, but she didn't have much time to worry herself with it.

"In five, four, three…" the cameraman said. He pointed to Abby as her cue.

"Good evening. My name is Abby Greene. You may be familiar with a series that I have been working on concerning teen suicide. Tonight, I bring you information of a bizarre, related story. It's the story of a young girl whose voice has not been heard for many years. Today, Becca Parsons speaks, and it's more powerful than you can imagine."

About the Author

When not writing or spending time with her family, you will find Lisa working in broadcast television as a media traffic manager. As a King's College graduate, Lisa attributes the enrichment of her writing to her exceptional teachers. Her love for mystery began at a very young age, when she first discovered Edgar Allan Poe and has been hooked ever since. Lisa resides in the coal region of the Northeast, with her husband, two wonderful sons and one crazy Jack Russell Terrier.

For your reading pleasure,
we invite you to visit our web
bookstore

WHISKEY CREEK PRESS
www.whiskeycreekpress.com

Made in the USA
Middletown, DE
25 August 2023

37145570R00136